TROUBLED DEATHS

The bright sunshine of Mallorca is overclouded by death, and Inspector Alvarez realises that wherever there are large sums of money involved there is motive for murder, and wherever there are strong emotions there is also motive for murder.

Inspector Alvarez has to dig deep into the expatriate way of life on this island—normally a relaxed atmosphere with leisurely wining and dining and perhaps the odd business deal—before he comes up with the answers he needs.

TROUBLED DEATHS

Roderic Jeffries

·BLACK·
DAGGER
·CRIME·

First published 1977
by
William Collins Sons & Co. Ltd

This edition 2004 by BBC Audiobooks Ltd
published by arrangement with
the author

ISBN 0 7540 8666 6

British Library Cataloguing in Publication Data available

Printed and bound in Great Britain by
Antony Rowe Ltd., Chippenham, Wiltshire

CHAPTER I

Caroline Durrel stood on the eastern arm of the harbour of Puerto Llueso and looked at the calm waters of the bay, the mountains which ringed them, and at the vivid, blue, cloudless sky. It was a scene of great beauty and timeless peace. She remembered, with an inward chuckle, old Colonel Atkin who had said to her, after his fourth brandy and while out of earshot of his very angular wife, 'You know, dammit, if it weren't for the people, this place'd be Arcadia.'

She turned and walked slowly back along the arm. She passed on her right the Club Nautico, the small Guardia post, the restaurant known for the quality of the fish it served and its prices, and the storage areas where fishermen left nets, boxes, and small pieces of equipment: she passed on her left yachts, motor cruisers, the ferries which sailed to Parelona beach, and finally the open, beamy fishing-boats with overhead stern lights fed by bottled gas. A young fisherman who had been swabbing down his boat watched her. His full bearded face was sensual and when he smiled at her there could be no doubt what he was thinking. Her answering smile showed appreciation of the compliment, but refusal of the accompanying proposition. He sighed as he resumed the swabbing.

Just beyond the point where the harbour arm joined the road there were two stalls, one of which was open. The man behind the counter looked sad and bored, so she bought a hotdog because she thought it might cheer him up a little to do some trade. He tried to shortchange her, but as she asked for the remaining five pesetas she decided he hadn't acted maliciously, merely from the force of habit.

As she bit into the hotdog, tomato ketchup squeezed out and slid down her chin. She laughed. A passing taxi almost crunched into the kerb. She began to cross the road and a French registered car slowed down and she waved her thanks, unaware of the fact that on the whole of the island he was the only French driver that day to show the slightest consideration towards a pedestrian.

On the far side of the road were several bars and when she came to the first one she sat at one of the tables set out on the pavement. It was mid-October, yet the sun was still warm and sitting out was a pleasure. A waiter, not as handsome as he believed himself, hurried out. 'Good morning, señorita,' he said, in heavily accented English. 'It is a most beautiful day, no?'

'Isn't it? . . . I'm meeting a friend here so I don't think I'll have anything until she arrives.'

'Maybe she shall be a long time?' he suggested, dropping his voice to what he considered to be a husky, intimate, thrilling tone.

'I don't think so. She's usually very punctual.' She made it clear that she would not be going with him to the local discotheque on Saturday night.

He shrugged his shoulders and left, because past experience of English visitors had made him lazy and he couldn't now be bothered to work in the pursuit of love.

She moved her chair round until she was directly facing the sun and then tilted up her head and closed her eyes. Back in England it was probably cold, wet, and windy, and everyone would be filled with the gloom of winter: out here it was warm, dry and calm, and winter was a season away.

After a time she heard the distant clacking of hard-soled shoes and she opened her eyes and looked to her left.

She was in time to see Mabel knock into the only other pedestrian within a hundred yards of her.

Mabel was wearing a pleated dress which might just have suited her twenty years before, her shoes were thick and graceless, and her hair was dishevelled. She came to the table and slumped down on to the chair. Her face was long and thin, which made her mouth appear to be far too full of teeth. Her eyes were a warm shade of blue and could have been one of her more attractive features, had she not so often squinted because she was short-sighted yet from a pathetic pride refused to wear glasses. 'Am I late? If I am, you can blame Norman. I tried to escape him, but he nobbled me and went on and on about that dog of his which is ill again. I told him, why not have the thing put down and save yourself all the trouble?'

Mabel would have meant the advice kindly, thought Caroline, but Norman could not have seen it like that. Mabel prided herself on speaking her mind. ('In that case,' someone had once said, 'she ought to keep dead quiet.') Locally, she was often referred to as Not-So-Jolly-Hockey-Sticks. It was not only an unkind nickname, it was also an inaccurate one. If she'd ever tried to play hockey, she'd have spent the entire game tripping over her own stick.

'Where's the waiter? They're getting lazier and lazier every week.' Mabel twisted round in her chair and waved at the opened door of the café. After a while, an elderly waiter wandered out.

'I'm going to have a brandy. What do you want, Carrie?'

'A sweet Martini, please.'

Mabel ordered in English since she refused to speak Spanish in case she made a mistake which left her open to ridicule. The waiter shuffled off back into the café.

Mabel, frowning as she screwed up her eyes, stared along the road in both directions. 'Have you seen Geoffrey this morning?'

'No. But then I've spent most of the time around the harbour.'

'He said he'd join us here for a drink. I wanted to ask him about something . . . ' She became silent, as if she couldn't be bothered, since only Caroline was present, to pursue the fiction that she'd only wanted to see Geoffrey to ask him something.

There were not many people in the world whom Caroline positively disliked: the friend of her father's who had just put his hand up her skirt when she was twelve, the maths master who'd been so sarcastic about her inability to scale the Himalayan peaks of cube roots, the drunken man who'd been driving the lorry which had skidded into her parents' car . . . And Geoffrey. He treated Mabel with an open contempt which made Caroline want to kick him where his pride would be worse hurt. How could any man behave like that towards a woman who loved him, however ridiculous she made herself?

The waiter brought them their drinks. Mabel added soda, tasted the brandy, and then said sharply: 'Is this one o three cognac?'

'Indeed, señora.'

'It's señorita. And I don't believe you. This tastes like something out of the bottom of the cheapest barrel.'

The waiter left, disinterested in her complaint, since the café's trade was largely with tourists.

Mabel spoke abruptly, her voice rising as it so often did when she was about to say something unwelcome. 'I saw Edward going into the baker's before I came here. I don't know what he was doing there in the middle of the morning.'

'I expect he was getting a couple of rolls for his lunch.'

She sniffed. 'I can't understand why he doesn't pull himself together and go back home and get a proper job.

I suppose he's too shy of any real work.'

'I've told you, his one love in life is boats and when he can't work on them he's not interested in anything else. Anyway, he's just finished working all hours of the day and night on a yacht. And d'you know something, when the owner of that yacht came out two days ago from England, he said he'd never seen such a good job!'

She looked at Caroline and suddenly her voice softened. 'Can't you see, Carrie, this island just isn't any good for a person like him.'

'Why ever not?'

'There's too much mañana, too much cheap drink, too little to do.'

And too many women willing to become friendly with Geoffrey. Poor Mabel, thought Caroline. What a different and happier life she might have lived if she'd fallen in love with a man who could have appreciated the person she really was under her clumsy, brash, abrasive exterior.

CHAPTER II

Ca'n Ritat stood at the far end of La Huerta de Llueso, just before the very rich, dark soil began to lighten and become more rock-strewn. Originally a three-hundred-year-old farmhouse, it had been very heavily restored and altered and, to the north, a servants' wing and garages – which thus enclosed a small courtyard – had been added: looking at it now it was difficult to realize it had once been a simple house. The garden was large, its fruitfulness guaranteed by the well in the south-west corner. The swimming pool was immediately beyond the lawn of Bermuda grass and beyond that was a field, enclosed by a dry-stone wall, in which grew orange, lemon, tangerine, almond, and fig trees, and whatever ground crops were in season. About a kilometre away the mountain rose up to fifteen hundred feet, thereby helping to reduce the severity of bad weather which came in from the north. An urbanizacion started at the foot of the mountain and this straggled part of the way up its slopes, until these became too precipitous: by some alchemy of bad taste, there was not one attractive house amongst them so that they tended to reduce the cold majesty of the harsh slopes.

Geoffrey Freeman, just six feet tall, still slim, dressed in cotton shirt and slacks and local Yanko sandals, stood by the side of the pool and looked back at the house. It was attractive, even though so heavily restored and added to and thereby denied its true identity, but the pleasure he gained from looking at it was measurable solely in financial terms. He had bought it for four million – the previous owner had been taken very seriously ill and his wife had been desperate to sell – and now it was worth at least seven million.

Money maketh man. Back in England he'd lived in a mortgaged semi-detached, his car had been a clapped-out Vauxhall, his clothes had come from a chain store, as had his wife's, and his two children had gone to the local comprehensive where they appeared to learn the law of the jungle and little else . . . Here, he was wealthy. He ran two cars, one a Mercedes, he had a seven-million-peseta home, and he employed a cook, a butler-cum-handyman, and a gardener, despite the fact that wages and insurance contributions had risen so high that many of the foreign residents had had to stop employing servants. He was the same man, but no longer unimportant. He knew everybody who was worth knowing, even if one or two of them did look down their noses at anyone not in Debrett. Lord and Lady Plichton had come to dinner more than once, as had Admiral Sir Alfred Postern who seemed to have won the last war single-handed . . .

Thank God Rose hadn't had the chance to come with him. She'd have messed everything up because there was a limit to what money could do. Look at the Zacaries, for example. She often entertained the local peasants, even to the extent of sitting down in the kitchen and drinking tea with them . . . Rose would have for ever been uneasy, wondering what was the correct etiquette for each situation, trying too hard to do the right thing and so ending up doing the wrong thing. He remembered how she'd looked the last time he'd seen her. Her dress had been faded and frayed at the hem, her apron torn, her face flushed, and her hair untidy.

She'd looked at him with that half antagonistic, half fearful expression which he'd come to know so well. 'You've not returned for lunch, have you? I've nothing in the house.'

'Stop panicking. I'm not eating here.'

'Then why have you come back?'

'I wanted my case.'

'Case? What case?'

'Suitcase.'

'What d'you want that for?'

Before he'd married her, he'd found her frequent air of bewildered puzzlement attractive, but after a few years of marriage it had become irritating because he realized it was simply the outward sign of an inability to cope with life. 'I need a suitcase to put a few things in. I'm leaving.'

'But where are you going and for how long? Why's the firm suddenly sending you away like this? They've never done it before.'

'The firm isn't sending me anywhere.'

'Geoff, I don't understand. What's happening?'

'I'm clearing out of a house which always smells of cabbage.'

'I haven't cooked cabbage in weeks,' she'd said, typically missing the point.

A movement on the looping road in the urbanizacion caught his interest and snapped his train of thought. Sun glinted on the glass of a car and he watched this ball of light continue on up to Cassell's house, where it stopped. That bastard! he thought with bitter anger. An internationally famous financier. Famous for what? Cassell had talked so knowingly of investing in options and commodities and making a fortune as the market rose. He'd invested heavily but had not gained a fortune because the silly bastard Cassell hadn't correctly identified the movements of the markets . . . Fifteen million it had cost him.

He saw Matilde come out of the courtyard and walk past the dog, which she patted, towards Orozco. She was from peasant stock, of course, but even so she was attractive in the overripe, sensual way that peasants sometimes were before they coarsened and went to seed. Under those tasteless clothes there must be a shapely body, ready to be fired up. Her husband Luis, couldn't do much firing. What had made her marry a man twice her age?

As she approached Orozco, he put his mattock on the ground and leaned on the handle. Give a Mallorquin a quarter of a chance to stop work and he seized it with both hands – provided the effort wasn't too great.

They talked for a while and Orozco laughed, which was a rare occurrence. Then she turned away and went back to the house. Orozco, still leaning on the mattock, watched her.

Freeman crossed the lawn and went along the gravel path. Orozco, although he must have heard the footsteps, made no effort to look as though he were busy.

Freeman stood in the centre of the path, hands on hips. 'Have you finished, then? Nothing more to do?' he asked roughly in English.

'Please, señor?' said Orozco, in his heavily accented English.

'I said, have you done all the work that needs doing?'

'No, señor.'

'Then why don't you bloody get on and do some of it?'

Orozco looked gravely at him and Freeman had the infuriating thought that Orozco was silently criticizing him for speaking so crudely. As if there were any other way of getting through his thick skull.

He turned round and walked towards the house. When he reached the courtyard the dog, tied to a chain, came out and barked at him. 'Shut up,' he shouted. He kicked a largish stone which was lying on the ground and more by chance than skill the stone hit the dog, which yelped.

He crossed the courtyard and went into the kitchen. Matilde was pounding something in a mortar and there were beads of sweat on her forehead: he watched the movement of her breasts. 'What's for lunch, then?'

'Pork chops with ali-oli, señor. I'm making the ali-oli.'

'There's nothing like the ali-oli you make. The only trouble is, after eating that much garlic I have to lay off kissing for a few hours.'

She concentrated on what she was doing and he became convinced she had not understood him. 'I said, after I've eaten your ali-oli with so much garlic in it I must try not to kiss a girl until the smell of garlic has gone.'

She picked up a plastic container of olive oil and added a few drops to the mixture.

They couldn't even understand if you spoke in words of one syllable, he thought, with brief contempt. 'Where's Luis, then?'

'He has to shop, señor, in Llueso.'

In other words, Luis was boozing at his favourite bar.

She worked the pestle once more and after a pause he left the kitchen and went along the hall to the sitting-room.

This was L-shaped, with the shorter arm separated from the longer by two archways. He'd bought the furniture with the house and that had been money well spent because even old Lady Glass, after a third brandy, had praised it in no uncertain terms. He crossed the Santa Barbara carpet to the cocktail cabinet and poured himself a gin and tonic. That reminded him that he'd half promised Mabel he'd have a drink with her and Caroline in the Port. Her real name was Mabel Striggs – which just about suited her since she looked the dried-up old spinster she was.

He sat on one of the softly upholstered armchairs. Some people couldn't take a hint if it was spelled out to them and Mabel was one such. Nothing he could say or do would stop her fluttering around him, to become all coy whenever the occasion warranted it . . .

He finished the gin and poured himself out another. Caroline could have been fun if only she'd been more sophisticatedly experienced – the world was made for the sharp, not the sweet.

As he sat on one side of a table in a back bar – here the prices were less than half those in the front bars – Edward Anson ran his fingers through his tangle of tight, curly brown hair. 'Yes, I saw Ramón this morning.'

Caroline studied his face. 'Well – aren't you going to tell me what it was all about? I've been so excited thinking about it.'

'You could have saved yourself the trouble.'

'Stop being so mournful. Really, Teddy, sometimes you try to paint everything so black. Where did you see him?'

'In his office. Being Ramón, he produced a bottle of expensive brandy and poured out a drink big enough to float a yacht.'

'But did he offer you any kind of a job? For heaven's

sake, that's what I want to hear about. He's such a nice man and I've been hoping and hoping on your behalf.'

'He didn't offer me a job. He offered me a partnership.'

She stared at him, utterly amazed. 'A . . . a partnership?' She shook her head. 'But that's much more than you ever dared hope for. Why, it's even more than I ever dreamt about! How can you sit there with a face a mile long, looking as if you'd just heard bad news?'

He shrugged his shoulders. He had a broad, very strongly-featured face, with light blue eyes that could often express more of his emotions than he wanted, and his complexion was weathered. It was easy to imagine him at sea, challenging wind and wave. 'It's not as simple as it sounds. Ramón will take me on because he reckons I'm good at the job and I'm English and so can deal with all the English-speaking people who want work carried out. He says I'd get a work permit because he can truthfully say I'd be doing a job no Spaniard could do because I've English contacts.'

'Then what isn't simple about that? I can see the nameplate on the side of the boatshed. "Mena and Anson, yacht designers and builders." You'll build a whole lot of super yachts and win all the big races and every rich yachtsman in the world will be rushing to you to get you to build him one.'

'Carrie, there's just one small condition to me being a partner. Ramón wants a million and a half pesetas to pay for the partnership.'

'Oh!' She stared at him. 'A million and a half . . . Is it worth that much?'

'Every time. If he'd doubled it to three million I'd still say it would be worth it. That place is a potential goldmine and he's a bloke who one can trust all the way . . . But a million and a half or three million, it doesn't make any difference. I don't know what that sort of money looks like.'

'You've just got to find it.'

'Under my pillow?' His tone became bitter. 'Carrie, I'd have to scratch around really hard to find ten thousand right now. A million and a half is like talking about me getting a degree in Greek.'

'Stop being so defeatist. There's always a way.'

'Not always, not in real life.'

'I just won't listen to you being gloomy. When an offer you've dreamed and dreamed about like this turns up it's because it's meant to happen. Therefore, it's going to happen.'

'It's a pity you don't run the world for it would be a much happier place if you did.'

She laughed. 'I don't know about that – I think it would most likely blow up in total confusion . . . But one thing's for sure. It's all arranged that you should join Ramón as a partner.'

'Maybe.'

'Maybe nothing.' She reached across the table and put her hand on his. 'Something will turn up, I can feel it in my bones. And they never, ever lie.'

CHAPTER III

At the time of their sudden deaths, Caroline's parents had been married for twenty-four years and during the whole of that time they had found no cause to regret anything. She had never heard them have a row and even their arguments had always been reasonably light-hearted. For years, she had thought all marriages were more or less like theirs and she had been quite shocked to discover that most weren't: shocked because she knew that happiness was more important than anything else in the world.

To be ready to, even to want to, believe the best of anyone and everyone was, in an age of growing cynicism, not only unusual but also not without possible dangerous consequences. But she was protected from such dangers by a keen sense of humour, a fund of common sense which allowed her to recognize rottenness when she met it, and an inner strength not immediately apparent. When the PC had called at the house to break the news that her parents had been killed in a very bad crash, she had naturally been totally shocked. But instead of giving way to her grief and demanding help, the kind of help which comes from accepting support from the strength of others, she had fought her own battles and, dry-eyed, had faced the world which had suddenly turned so black.

When it was all over, she'd decided to give herself a complete break by returning for the winter to where she and her parents had had the happiest of their many holidays. As any cynic would have told her, this must prove disastrous – the one unvarying rule of travel is, never return . . . And on top of that, there would be all the painful associations . . . She returned and found the peace and beauty she had remembered and when she thought about her parents it was not with a throat-tightening sorrow, but with a sense of thankfulness that they had been permitted to die together after having known so much love together.

She'd first met Mabel Cannon at a cocktail party given by an ex-property tycoon between wives. She'd noticed the lumpy, awkward, badly-dressed woman who sat in a cane chair at the far end of the immense sitting-room and typically she had immediately felt sorry for this person to whom nobody could be bothered to speak. She'd gone straight over and introduced herself. Initially, Mabel had been suspicious of Caroline's motives, but her sincerity had been too obviously genuine to be misinterpreted, even by a very lonely woman who was always, in the company of the rich, the successful, the good-looking, and the well connected, all too painfully aware of her own very limited attractions.

Her suspicions allayed, Mabel had responded to the younger woman's friendship with a gratitude that could have been embarrassing. Had it been directed towards anyone else, there would undoubtedly have been speculation whether there was a lesbian base to it, but not even the sharpest tongue in the area – and few came sharper – suggested such a thing. So great was Mabel's gratitude that had Caroline gone to her and asked for a loan of one and a half million pesetas for herself, she would have given it without question. But, knowing this, Caroline felt in honour bound to explain precisely what she wanted the money for.

Mabel shifted in the armchair and crossed her legs, careless about the way in which the pleated skirt revealed her thick thighs. She fiddled with the arm of the chair, where one of the cords of the material had frayed. She was no more concerned about the way in which the house was furnished than the way in which she dressed: most of the furniture had been bought in a second-hand shop or from people leaving the island and nothing matched, much was dingy. 'Who told you about this partnership?'

'Teddy did, of course. You can't think what a wonderful chance it is for him, Mabel. All his life . . .'

'Why should Mena offer him a partnership?'

'He's a first class worker and knows everything about boats.'

'But does he ever work? Whenever I see him, he's lounging around the place, doing nothing.'

'Of course you haven't seen him actually working as you've never been in the boatyard and hardly ever go along the harbour. When you see him in the Port, he's taking a break.'

'Seven hours' break and one hour's work a day.'

Caroline laughed. 'You're just prejudiced! I'm sure you don't believe anyone works who isn't in an office. Teddy's not cut out for that sort of life. He's always loved boats and his one burning ambition has always been to have his own business. Now Ramón's offered him the chance and he's over the moon with excitement.'

'He'll never be given a work permit.'

'Yes, he will. All Ramón has to prove is that Teddy will be doing a job a Mallorquin can't and since he'll be dealing with the English-speaking foreigners that's obvious. Another thing, the business employs several Mallorquins so it'll be even easier . . . Look, why don't you come along to the boatyard with me and see what he's doing now. It's fascinating to see the kind of work he does.'

'I don't like boats. They make me seasick.'

Caroline laughed again. 'The one he's working on now would have a bit of a job! It's in a cradle up on dry land. Come on, let's go and see him when we've finished our drinks.'

'Why are you going on and on about it?'

'Because I want you to realize he isn't the layabout you seem to think he is.'

'Jason told me he's lazy and hopelessly incompetent.'

'You know that Jason doesn't like anyone who doesn't dress in silk shirts and manicure his nails twice a day. And I happen to know why Jason's talking like that. He got Teddy to revarnish the deck of his yacht and now he won't pay up, but keeps making excuses and inventing complaints. It's terrible when you think that Jason's as rich as Croesus and Teddy hasn't a penny.'

'If he hasn't any money, he won't be able to pay the million and a half, will he?'

'No . . . Not unless he can borrow it.'

'No bank's going to be that stupid. Give him one and a half million and he'd be out of the country as fast as he could run.'

'That's being ridiculous.'

'You haven't learned what men are like.'

'But Teddy could be trusted with a hundred million . . . Mabel, if you can, will you lend it to him? It could all be done legally and if you're still so worried the money could be paid directly to Ramón. Teddy would give you full interest and so you'd be benefiting and you'd be giving him the chance of a lifetime.'

'The chance to go on drifting.'

'Don't be so prejudiced . . .'

'I've seen dozens like him. They come out here because the drink's cheap and the women are even cheaper and they just drift around expecting to live on charity. There's a very crude word for them – beach-bums.'

'That's not Teddy.'

'No? Then why didn't he have the courage to come and ask me for the money face to face instead of making you do it?'

'He doesn't even know I've asked. It was entirely my idea.'

'Nonsense! He's hiding behind your skirts, but you're far too nice to realize it. You're too kind-hearted. Some-one's only got to invent a new hard-luck story for you to get all worried and upset about him. You must stop believing everything you hear and learn to be suspicious. If you don't, one of these days you're going to find out the truth about men in the nastiest way.' Her mouth twisted into bitter lines.

Caroline had always had tremendous sympathy for the underprivileged, but her sympathy was far from uncritical, as Mabel supposed. She had the intuitive ability to be able to sort out those whose misfortunes were due to circumstances beyond their control from those whose misfortunes were due to their own inadequacies, which could be overcome if only they fought. It was Edward Anson's fighting spirit which had so appealed to her from the moment she had first met him.

The world had given him a tough ride. His parents had been poor and the marriage bitterly unhappy and he had become a shuttlecock of emotional contention between them long before he could really appreciate that fact. His memories of childhood — he seldom spoke about those times — were of rows and causeless blows. Just before his seventh birthday, his father had gone off with another woman to leave his wife penniless. She had moved to Hampshire where she had obtained a job as housekeeper in a house which bordered the River Test. There, Anson had found the world of boats.

He was not an articulate man, except where boats were concerned, and therefore could not readily explain the psychological meaning boats had come to have for him, but Caroline was certain that for him they were freedom from all the emotional unhappiness found ashore. A boat sailed one away from the land where a man would try to prove his manhood by subjugating a woman: at sea, only the wind and the waves were truly powerful and they were neutral.

When his mother had died, after a painful illness, he had had to leave the house by the river. He'd drifted, in the sense that he had moved from job to job and place to place, but his goal had always been crystal-clear to him. On a May day he had landed in Palma from the Barcelona ferry and three weeks after that he had wandered into Puerto Llueso. He had stood on the front and looked at the harbour and he had suddenly known that here was where his destination had lain from the beginning. He had gone to the two boatyards and the three boat-builders in the Port and had asked for a job and each one had refused him. The next week he'd visited them again and they'd refused again: and each week after that. He'd swallowed his pride – of which he had far too much – and he'd badgered English yacht-owners, whom he stupidly despised just because they were, by definition, wealthy, asking, pleading to be given some work. One man, attracted by the chance of having the work done cheaply, had offered him the job of rubbing down and varnishing the deck and super-structure of a thirty-foot cruiser. He'd worked on that boat with all the care of a restorer working on an old master, not only because he wanted to create an impression, but also because where boats were concerned he was a per-fectionist. The owner had been duly impressed, by the standard of workmanship and by the reasonable size of the bill.

When the boatyards were busy, no one worried that a few odd jobs were carried out by a foreigner who had no work permit. But as the world went into economic reces-sion, the number of yachts in the Port became fewer and owners of those which remained cut back on the work they had carried out on them. Then, the men who ran the boatyards began to concern themselves with the work they were not getting because a foreigner was undercutting their charges. This was how Ramón Mena had first met Anson.

Mena had intended to lay a denunciation, which would quickly have removed the nuisance. But he also had a passion for boats and when he saw the work Anson was doing he realized that here was someone after his own heart. He delayed the denunciation and spoke to Anson about many things, and the upshot was instead of having him removed from the island, he offered him a partnership. For Anson, it was a dream desperately trying to come true.

Caroline walked along the front, past the bars where a gin and tonic cost fifty to sixty pesetas, and then down one of the cross streets to a back bar where it cost twenty. Anson had not yet arrived, so she sat at one of the tables. The barman came out from behind the counter – normally he refused to serve the tables – and asked her how things were and how was she? She understood enough of what he said to reply that she was fine. She asked him if she could have a coffee.

She saw Anson cross the square and then wait in the shadow of a palm tree for a couple of cars to pass. He was strong, she thought, like an oak tree, but like an oak tree he had not learned to bend to the wind. He refused to practise discretion, to temper his instinctive and baseless dislike of wealth and heritage, to stop preparing to bite the hand which might feed him . . .

He opened the door, stepped into the café, came to the table, and sat. He ran a hand, stained with grease, through his mop of curls and then rubbed the tip of his nose on the back of his hand. His craggy face was browned by sun and wind so that there was the look of a gypsy about him.

'I could murder a brandy. Have you ordered anything, Carrie?'

'Pedro's bringing me a coffee.'

He turned and called for a large brandy. 'The wind's a bit of a bite to it today. I've been reeving some new rigging and got bloody chilled.'

'Why on earth haven't you been wearing a sweater?'

'Didn't think I'd need one,' he answered uninterestedly. He brought a pack of Ducados from his pocket and offered her a cigarette.

'Teddy, I . . .' She stopped. She was a little afraid how

he would react to what she was going to say. She leaned forward to light her cigarette on the match he had just struck.

'Well?'

'Please don't look at me like that.'

'I'm wondering just what in the hell you've been up to. When you've got that expression on your face, it's got to be something dramatic.'

'It isn't really. It's just . . . Teddy, I've been having a word with Mabel.'

'A word about what?'

'Well, I . . . I tried to persuade her to lend you the money you so need.'

'You did what?' His voice thickened. 'What d'you think you . . .'

'I knew you'd never ask her yourself. And you said the banks won't help. I just thought she might lend it to you . . . Teddy, it's no good sitting back on your dignity and dislikes. You may never get a chance like this again and you've got to do everything you possibly can to try to grab it. If she'd lend the money to you . . .'

'You should have saved your breath for cooling porridge: and kept your nose out of my affairs. I wouldn't ask that old bitch for the time.'

'She's not that kind of person at all when you get to know her.'

'Pass me by on that pleasure.'

'You're being very stupid.'

'Now there's one thing I'm really good at.'

'You can say that again sometimes!' She shook her head. 'Look, all I was trying to do was help you, so don't jump down my throat too hard.'

'But can't you see that she's the last person to ask for anything?'

'No, I can't. Underneath, she's really quite nice and kind.'

'Carrie, you're soft enough to see a Prince Charming inside every frog.'

'Everything's so much nicer like that. And quite often there really is one, you know.'

'OK, Cinderella.'

She smiled.

The bartender brought the coffee and brandy. He asked Anson how he was and Anson answered in rough, but serviceable Spanish that things weren't too bad.

After stirring in a spoonful of sugar and sipping the coffee, she put down the cup and said: 'If Mabel won't help, you've got to find some other way of getting the money and I think I've found one. The banks won't lend it to you now because you can't offer them any security. But suppose you put down half a million and then only asked for the remaining million? You'd be showing them how you believe in yourself and that means a lot. I think they'd let you have it.'

'If I'd half a million, I'd have already tried that.'

'I've that much which I could bring out from England.'

'No,' he said sharply.

'Why not? It's not as if I wouldn't get it all back. And if it would make the bank lend you the rest . . .'

'I'm not taking a peseta from you.'

'But this is your chance in a lifetime.'

'It's the chance I've longed for from the day I first saw a dinghy in a stiff wind tacking across the Test with her gunwale almost under and the sail as tight as a drumhead. But I'm still not touching a peseta of yours.'

'You can be terribly stubborn.'

'I was born plain, bloody awkward.'

'Then I'll go back and ask Mabel again. Maybe I could get her in a more sympathetic mood.'

'I've told you once. Keep your nose out of my business.'

She was not upset by his rudeness. She understood that it concealed emotions which he did not wish to be identified.

CHAPTER IV

Luis Blanco had grey hair, a leathery, creased complexion, dark brown eyes, and a wide, thick-lipped mouth. He walked with a slight limp which became pronounced whenever he was tired: a .303 bullet had nicked his femur – a fraction to the right and it would have shattered the bone, perhaps beyond repair. He wore a badly fitting grey suit which hung about him and the collar of his shirt was so large that it gaped away from his neck and the tie sagged: his beret had once been brown, but now it was more nearly black. He carried a medium-sized suitcase, one corner of which was badly worn so that the middle layer of cardboard showed through the plastic.

He stopped half-way along the drive, put down the suitcase, and waited patiently for Orozco to finish the work he was doing: one hurried only for birth or death. He took a large red handkerchief from his pocket and blew his nose, so loudly that the dog in the courtyard barked a couple of times.

Orozco finished what he was doing, dropped the mattock to one side, and plodded along the side of a flower-bed to the drive. 'Are you off now, then?'

'Hernandez's brother is driving his lorry into Palma and he says he'll take me.'

'Have you heard how your brother is?'

'They say he is very ill. Perhaps he is dying.'

'Please God they are wrong and there will be no bells

and long-faced priests.'

Blanco shrugged his shoulders with a fatalistic acceptance of whatever the future might be. A tomato seed sewn in January grew into a plant which fruited in June and died in October and no man could alter that rhythm: death came when it wished, not when man willed. 'I've spoke to Matilde and said I must be with my brother until he gets better or dies. Perhaps I will be there many days. See all goes well, Lopez.'

'Don't worry, Luis, I will look after her.'

Blanco nodded. He blew his nose again, hawked, spat. 'I'll be on my way.' He picked up the suitcase.

'God go with you,' said Orozco. He watched Blanco walk to the end of the drive, pass through the gateway, and turn right on to the camino.

He went back along the drive and from behind an oleander bush he picked up a leather porron and drank some wine from it. He wondered what Barcelona looked like now. He remembered it as a city of hatred and revenge, where God had been forgotten and the Devil ruled in high state.

As he replaced the porron, Matilde came out of the courtyard and walked towards him. She was beautiful, he thought without lust. She smiled at him and said: 'I suppose you saw Luis a moment ago?'

'Yes. He told me that Hernandez is taking him into Palma. He says his brother is very ill.'

'Did he ask you to look after me?'

'Yes.'

'He always used to fuss and now he fusses more than ever. Of course I shall be alright. I am not a child.'

He said nothing. It was obvious to anyone that she was not a child.

'And he is ridiculous to think I am too friendly with Garcia. I talk and laugh with Garcia when I meet him, but that is all. I said to Luis, "Do you think Garcia can be anything to me but someone to laugh with and talk to? You are my husband. He is just a boy!"'

Her friendship with Garcia was no concern of his so long as Garcia did not try to come to Ca'n Ritat whilst Luis was away. And no matter what, no woman in full bloom was going completely to ignore the admiration of a handsome man of her own age. Still, it was right a husband should be jealous.

She was disappointed when he remained silent. 'The señor wants lettuce for lunch,' she said, speaking rather sullenly, 'so pick me two.'

'Two?'

'He's having company.' She was far too cheerful by nature ever to remain annoyed for long and now she giggled. 'Special company, he calls her.'

'What does that mean? Another whore?'

'Some of 'em dress more like grand ladies.'

'The more paint, the bigger whore.'

'And how would you know?' she asked archly. 'Or did you do much more than just fight in the war?'

'If I did it was all a long time ago.'

'Just as well! . . . You ought to get married again.'

'I've suffered enough for one life.'

She laughed. 'Come on, you old misery, how about those lettuces?'

He left and walked back to the long kitchen garden. He chose the two thickest-hearted plants and pulled them, knocked off the earth from their roots against the heel of his shoe, then stripped off some of the outside leaves. He returned to the drive and handed her the lettuces.

He watched her walk back to the house, hips swinging.

Freeman briefly looked at his plain gold Previn wristwatch. Ten minutes late, which for this island was early. A woman pushing a pram, began to cross the road without looking and he hooted, making her start. The locals had the traffic sense of half-witted Hottentots, he thought with sharp annoyance.

He turned on to the front road and went along past the end of the central island to swing round so that he could drive back up to the café. He passed one of the hotels and then saw Veronica at a table at the first café. She was staring to her right, trying to identify him as he drove out from the Llueso road. She'd missed him because she'd no idea he had a Mercedes.

He braked to a halt and still she didn't look round. She was wearing a very tight blouse and a skirt which was too short: she had used over-much make-up. Flashy, he thought, but flashiness had always held a perverse attraction for him.

He pressed the switch and the nearside front window wound down to the low hum of an electric motor. 'Hi, there! Looking for someone?'

Startled, she turned. She noticed the car and although she tried to hide the fact, he could see she was impressed by its opulence.

'I'm going for a drive. Care to come along?' he asked facetiously.

'You're late, Geoff, and I was beginning to think . . .' She stopped.

She'd begun to think he couldn't be bothered. Probably she'd been all ready to bitch if and when he did finally turn up, but now he'd arrived in a vast Mercedes she was too awed to say anything much. 'Well, are you coming my way?'

She stood up, crossed the pavement, climbed into the front seat and as she settled down she looked back along the pavement towards the hotel. Hoping her friend could see her riding off in the lap of luxury, he thought. 'You'd better do the safety-belt up. It's obligatory and if the police catch you with it undone they fine you some fantastic sum of pesetas.'

She clipped the belt around herself. 'The police out here scare me, with all their guns. D'you know, when we were coming to the hotel from the airport we saw a couple of policemen with sub-machine guns.'

'You're quite safe. They only shoot tourists in leap year.'

She giggled. 'I must remember not to come out then.'

He put the gear lever to drive and drew out into the road, careless of an oncoming Seat 600 which had to brake quite sharply and noisily.

'Where are we going for lunch, Geoff? That place in Palma you were talking about where the food's so special?'

He accelerated to the K-junction, then braked heavily for the Llueso road. He was in a fast car, so he always drove fast. 'I had a change of mind. I thought it would be more fun this time to have a meal at my place so I told the cook to lay on a really nice cold meal.'

'Have you got a cook?'

'That's what she calls herself, but most of the time she could fool me. They're all the same out here. Give 'em a cupful of beans and an ounce of belly of pork and they knock up a meal for half a dozen peasants, but give 'em decent food and like as not they'll ruin it.'

'If you've a cook, I suppose you've quite a big house, Geoff.'

'I wouldn't ever call it that,' he said, in a throwaway tone of voice. He could almost hear her mind working: expensive car, a cook, a big house . . .

They left the Port and he drove very fast along the straight Llueso road, blasting past a couple of small cars which had strayed into the centre. 'Most of 'em still think they're in donkey carts,' he said. 'They spend their time at the wheel asleep.'

'But aren't the donkey carts fun? I think it's all so romantic.'

'Provided you like donkeys.'

'I suppose you've been around the world too much to see it like I do?'

'I've been around,' he agreed.

She sighed. 'I've always wanted to travel a lot. As I said to Di only yesterday, there's nothing like travel to show you how the other people live. And that has to be a good thing, doesn't it?'

It was extraordinary how most people led cliché lives and could only think and talk in clichés. Rose had been like that. Just for a moment, he wondered where Rose and the two children were right then. Not driving around in a Mercedes, that was for sure.

When they turned into Ca'n Ritat's drive, she said: 'Is this where you live? But it's lovely. So . . . so local. And look at all the flowers in the garden. There aren't really any flowers left in the garden at home. My dad's a terribly keen gardener and if he could see this he'd go green with envy. I suppose you spend all day in the garden?'

'Me? Why should I get my hands dirty when I employ a gardener to get his?'

'You've got a gardener! . . . He must be a good one.'

He stopped the car. 'He's OK on vegetables, but pretty bloody useless on anything else. Can't grow English seeds even when I tell him exactly how. And you're not going to believe this, but he ignores the weather and won't plant out until it's the right Saint's Day for whatever it is he's planting!' He looked at her and saw she was puzzled, not having understood the reason for his scorn. Peasant-minded.

She opened her door, released the seat-belt, and stepped out. The dog, which had come forward to the extent of its chain, barked. 'Belt up,' shouted Freeman.

'What's his name?' she asked.

'God knows.' He picked up a stone, threw it, and missed.

'Why d'you throw that?'

'Because the bloody mongrel's good for nothing but barking. I've told the Blancos to get rid of it, but like the rest of the people on this island they never do what they're told.'

She walked over to the dog, spoke to it, and patted its head. The tail began to wag. 'He's not nearly as fierce as he sounds. Are you, poochy? Geoff, he's really friendly.'

'So what am I supposed to do about that? Take it to bed with me?'

She gave it a last pat. She wasn't sure if she liked Geoff as much as she'd thought she would. Then she looked at the house, the garden, and the car, and decided that one couldn't have everything.

'Leave it alone and come and have a drink.' He led the way along the gravel path which ran round the side of the house, past the front door, to the patio.

'You've even got a swimming pool!' she exclaimed, as she came round the corner of the house and saw the pool for the first time.

'The water's heated, so you can have a dip.'

'No, I can't. I haven't brought a costume.'

'Why should that stop you?'

She giggled.

They went from the patio into the sitting-room. She had expected comfort, but not the degree of luxury she saw. The furniture, furnishings, silver, and paintings, all spoke of considerable wealth. His wife would be able to dress in expensive clothes and drive around in her own Mercedes ... Di would choke with envy ...

'What'll you drink?' he asked.

'I wouldn't mind a very little gin and tonic.'

'On this island, no one's ever heard of a little gin.' He

crossed to the cocktail cabinet. 'Park your bottom. There's no extra charge for sitting.'

She sat on the settee, crossed her legs, and with great affectation tugged her skirt an inch further down her thighs.

Matilde came into the sitting-room and looked with brief curiosity, and perhaps a suggestion of criticism, at Veronica, then said in Spanish:

'Everything is ready for the meal, señor.'

'All right.'

'I have put on the table chicken and ham and potato salad and lettuce . . .'

'OK.'

'Should there be anything more you want, señor . . .'

'I'll shout.'

She left.

'Was that the cook?' asked Veronica, and although she wasn't aware of the fact her voice had sharpened slightly.

'She does the cooking, sure. But like I said earlier, the only thing she can cook well are beans.'

Then there was a readily available excuse for sacking her at the first opportunity, thought Veronica, who had been disagreeably surprised to see how attractive Matilde was.

He poured out the drinks, gave her one, and then went and sat in one of the armchairs and not on the settee with her as she'd obviously expected. He talked casually, lightly, and maliciously, about the people who lived in the area, making it seem as if the rich and the titled were his constant and boon companions. He gave her a second and even stronger gin and tonic and after handing her the glass he let his hand slide along her arm. She smiled coyly at him, was clearly very surprised, even disconcerted, when he did not follow up his advance, but retired to his chair. She was not used to very strong drinks on an empty stomach and after a third one she began to tell him about how she'd always wanted to live on a sunny island.

A grandfather clock struck the half hour. He crossed to the settee and she put her nearly empty glass down on a piecrust table and waited. He kissed her with skilful passion and began a pincer sweep of his hands. She did not retreat and when his advances threatened to become a full frontal attack, she murmered: 'Not here, Geoff darling.'

'What's the matter?'

'Someone might come in. Your cook . . .'

'I told her to keep right out of it.'

'Let's go upstairs?'

'You're not living in Clapham now,' he said cryptically, as he began a flanking movement.

She lifted herself up to aid him in his task and then suddenly thought she heard something. 'What's that?' She instinctively grabbed his right hand which was making a final tactical withdrawal.

'My hand. What in the hell d'you think it is?'

'But I heard something go bang.'

He suggested what she had heard and she giggled and let go of his hand in a sign of total surrender. She began to unbutton him.

A high-pitched voice cried out: 'Oh, my God!'

They turned, their hands momentarily frozen in position. When Veronica saw Mabel, she gave a muted scream. She released him, made a grab for her pants and tried to pull them up from her ankles, rolled off the settee and landed on the floor with a thump that made her gasp.

'Oh, my God!' cried Mabel for the second time. Her face was working and her expression was one of tortured shock: she kept looking away and then back at the two of them.

'What in the hell are you doing here?' demanded

Freeman. He began to button himself up.

'You . . . you . . .' Mabel closed her eyes and shivered. 'You invited me to lunch,' she wailed. She suddenly began to sneeze: long-drawn-out sneezes which shook her whole body.

'Not today, for Pete's sake.'

She opened her eyes and managed to catch her sneezing long enough to say: 'You told me today.' Tears welled out of her blue eyes and coursed down her roughened cheeks. 'You asked me for Thursday.'

'Friday.'

'You said Thursday.'

'Thursday, Friday, tomorrow, today, God Almighty, who the hell cares now?' muttered Veronica frantically. She rolled over, came to her feet, bent down to pull up her pants, overbalanced, and slid so that her backside stuck up at a sharp angle and she was reminded of the fact that her bottom had recently become rather pimply. She began to sob from humiliation.

'If there's one single way of getting things wrong and creating a snarl-up, you'll find it,' he said to Mabel.

'Geoffrey, I promise you . . .' Mabel sneezed. 'You did tell me Thursday.'

'Friday.'

'What's the matter if you said bloody Sunday?' screamed Veronica. 'She's here now, isn't she?'

They ignored her. 'You asked me for Thursday, today,' said Mabel and she suddenly began to moan.

Veronica tried to get up, forgot her pants were still around her ankles, and collapsed sideways, knocking over the table on which her glass had been. The remaining gin and tonic splattered over her stomach.

'You told me Thursday,' cried Mabel. She turned and ran out of the room into the hall. Seconds later, they heard the front door slam shut.

Veronica pulled off her pants, stood up and roughly mopped the gin and tonic off her stomach with them, then grabbed the rest of her clothes.

They heard a car engine start up and the car, engine revving too high, drive off.

'I once knew a man,' said Freeman, 'who told me he owed his success in life to living by the motto, "Always expect the unexpected." I guess he must have known Mabel.'

She zipped up her skirt. 'I said we should have gone upstairs,' she cried shrilly.

'But who was to foresee this kind of a visitation?' He smiled. 'I'll tell you one thing for sure. We've given her either nightmares or ideas for the next month.'

She pulled on her blouse and buttoned it up. 'Take me back to the hotel.'

'Stop panicking, remember this is Mallorca where the only inexcusable sin is to be frustrated. Have another drink and forget it.'

'You made me look a cheap tart.'

Nature had long ago forestalled him. 'I know it was rather unfortunate, but it's all over and done with now.'

She scrumpled up her pants and brassière in her right hand. 'Are you going to take me?'

'I promise you she won't come back for a repeat performance.' He walked over and kissed her. His right hand began another advance.

She slapped his face with her left hand and hurried over to the French windows and pulled them open. Once outside, she ran along the path and across to the car. The dog, tail wagging, came out to the length of its chain, but she ignored it so it barked a couple of times to remind her of its presence. Freeman, hurrying to catch up with her, booted the dog in its ribs and it howled as it fled back into its kennel, made from a 150-litre drum.

CHAPTER V

Friday was a dull day. Clouds came in on a westerly wind after dusk and by daybreak they covered the sky: they threatened rain, but this only fell up in the mountains. Llueso, which in sunshine was a place of timeless peace became forlorn and even a trifle shabby, to which a touch of melancholy was added by all the closed shutters. A fisherman, selling from a battered old Citroën van fish caught the previous night, blew a conch shell to attract the housewives' attention. A knife-grinder blew a set of Pipes of Pan to advertise his trade. An umbrella-mender unhurriedly sought work, sitting down on the front step of a house when he found it.

On the west side of the square people were selling caged goldfinches, canaries, and zebra finches, and quail, guinea pigs, rabbits and chickens, the chickens that were ready for eating being hobbled and left sprawled out on the ground, from which undignified position they watched uncomplainingly. On the north-east side women sold lettuces, sweet potatoes, potatoes, cabbages, cauliflowers, and early oranges. On the south-east side the café had set out twenty tables and a number of these were occupied, some by tourists, others by foreign residents who studied the tourists with amused condescension.

Freeman signalled to a waiter, who came across to their table. 'The same again,' he ordered.

'I really don't think I ought to have another one,' said Mary Pollard.

'That's right, you shouldn't,' agreed her husband.

'I swore last night I'd be dry for a fortnight. Oh my God,

did I have a head this morning when I woke up!' she sighed.

'You must have put too much soda in the brandy,' said Freeman.

'It was at Pete and Corinna's and you know what they're like – the cheapest plonk from the barrel put into a bottle. It's a wonder no one's died from the stuff they pour.'

'If it's that bad, why go there?'

'One's got to do something to make the time pass. And on top of their frightful booze, I had Chris talking to me all night. That man could bore a microphone silly.'

'I always feel sorry for Madge,' said Pollard, 'having to put up with him every day.'

'I hear she keeps some of her nights free, though,' said Freeman.

'You shouldn't listen to malicious gossip,' said Mary.

The waiter returned and put fresh glasses in front of them, took away the empty ones.

Mary drank. 'That's better. I'm beginning to feel I might live.'

Freeman raised his glass and then suffered a pain which sliced through his stomach with such intensity that he drew in his breath. Then it was gone.

Pollard looked curiously at him. 'Is anything wrong, old man?'

'It just felt as if something had gone off bang in my guts. I suppose a muscle suddenly kicked up. Or it's old age galloping in.'

'Who's she supposed to be going around with?' asked Mary.

'Who's who?' asked Freeman.

'For heaven's sake, who were we talking about? Madge, of course.'

'Didn't you tell me not to listen to malicious gossip?'

'Quite right. But once you've heard it, you've a duty to

pass it on. Is it Bunny?'

'I reckon he's far too much of a rabbit to have an affair with her.'

'Oh, God, Geoff, can't you do better than that? . . . Was it Bunny? I wouldn't be at all surprised. After all, if you're Madge and you've got Chris as a husband you can't afford to be over particular.'

Freeman opened his mouth to speak and the pain hit him again and this time lasted much longer. He grasped his stomach and sweat prickled his forehead.

'Geoff,' she said, 'what is the matter with you?'

He spoke very slowly. 'The pain's come back . . .' Miraculously, as he spoke it vanished.

'D'you think it's appendicitis? Exactly whereabouts is it hurting?'

'Try to keep the conversation reasonably clean,' said Pollard.

With sharp resentment, Freeman realized that they thought he was dramatizing the pain.

'Would you like a brandy instead of that gin? I've always said that out here even the best local gin will burn holes in tablecloths.'

A third pain rocketed across his stomach, lunging out in all directions, and he knew he was going to be sick before long.

'If it is appendicitis you'll find the pain begins to concentrate on the right-hand side,' said Mary. 'Or is it the left? I never can remember. But even a local doctor should know that.'

He stood up very slowly, holding on to the table for support.

'D'you think we ought to run you back home?' she asked.

'There's no need for that.' He noticed their looks of relief. He took two one-hundred-peseta notes from his pocket. 'Will you pay the waiter for me?'

He left them. He walked to the steps, down them, and then the twenty feet to his parked Mercedes. He sat down behind the wheel, started the engine, backed out and turned.

He had to wait at the 'Stop' sign on the Palma road and here the fourth pain filled his belly with raging fire. He vomited with explosive force. A car had pulled up behind him and the driver of this, becoming increasingly impatient, began to toot the horn.

The doctor didn't speak after leaving the bedroom until he was downstairs in the sitting-room. 'Señora,' he said to Matilde, 'I must call in a specialist from Palma.'

'Then the señor is very ill?' she asked worriedly.

'Ill enough,' he answered grimly. 'Now tell me exactly all that happened.'

She explained how Santiago, a relation on her mother's side, had wanted to drive out on to the Palma road and how this huge foreign car had just remained in the way so that in the end he had got out of his car to tell the driver to move. He had found the señor doubled up and retching, so – like any Mallorquin ready to help in trouble – he had pushed the señor to one side and driven the señor's car to the house so that the doctor could be called.

The doctor, deep in thought, stared out through one of the windows.

'Is he . . . Is he going to live, señor?' she asked.

'Ask God, not me, señora, but right at this moment I think even His reply might well be slightly ambiguous.' He turned. 'Has he been out of the island recently? Perhaps to India?'

'He has been nowhere for many months and then he went only to the Peninsula.'

'I see. Well, the symptoms are very similar to those of cholera.'

'Mother of God!' she cried.

'There's no need to panic,' he said testily. 'If it is cholera, we may save him and in any case there's no cause for you to think you're next in line for the coffin. Is there a telephone in the house?'

'Yes, señor.'

'Then I'll ring Palma . . . Is the señor a wealthy man?'

'He has many, many millions of pesetas.'

'Good. He is going to need some of them right now.'

Orozco hawked and spat. He rubbed the back of his earth-stained hand across his chin, which had not been shaved that morning. 'There was cholera in Barcelona when I was there.'

'And did the people die of it, Lopez?' Matilde asked.

'Like flies.'

'Sweet Mary preserve us . . . What about Luis? Do I write and tell him?'

'Wait and see,' he answered, with a peasant's stoic acceptance of whatever fortune fate had in store.

Freeman suffered dehydration, yet he could not quench his thirst because to drink was to vomit. He suffered sural spasms and intense abdominal pains. His face became pinched and his eyes sunken. He knew he was desperately ill and yet the initial panic of this knowledge gave way to a feeling of indifference.

After a while the symptoms miraculously vanished. In the place of indifference came a growing hope and then a belief that he would live. But just as his belief became certainty, the symptoms returned in ever more bitter form. He lost consciousness for increasing periods of time, his circulation began to fail, and he suffered convulsions.

Finally, he entered a coma and died, not long after the medical tests showed that he had not been suffering from cholera.

CHAPTER VI

Inspector Alvarez awoke, but for a moment he did not open his eyes. The end of a siesta was a sad time, more especially when one had drunk and smoked a little too much beforehand and one's mouth tasted like . . . It was better not to seek an adequate simile.

A fly buzzed above his head. Why? Why expend the energy when it could have settled upside down on the ceiling and slept? He opened his eyes and looked up and tried to see the fly, but because the shutters were closed the light was too poor. He checked the time and the hands said it was half past four. What had woken him so early?

The fly landed on his nose, which was broad enough to make a landing space for a squadron of flies. He blew upwards and the fly took off, to resume its ridiculous buzzing. He yawned, then stretched out his short, powerful arms. Tomorrow, he thought with deep pleasure, was Sunday and therefore he would not have to come to the Guardia post to work.

After a while he stood up, crossed to the window, and pushed open the shutters. He looked down at the narrow street and watched a young woman walk along and there was something about her lithe movements which he found erotic. Then it occured to him that these days most young women whether standing or walking struck him as erotic. He sighed. The tragedy of middle age was that a man still dreamed, but the volcano in his belly had died down to just a little camp fire.

The telephone rang. He ignored it. An elderly woman, stooping and dressed all in black, followed the sensuous young woman along the road. How many years had she been in black to mark her husband's death? The old people still followed the traditions, but the younger ones scorned them and they'd be in very short, brightly coloured skirts before their poor husbands had had time to talk things over with St Peter. A man's death was crowned with thorns, even if in life he had escaped a pair of horns.

The phone was still ringing so reluctantly he returned to the desk and picked up the receiver. 'Yeah?'

'Where have you been?' demanded the captain. 'Fast asleep, I suppose, snoring your head off?'

'Señor,' said Alvarez, with polite firmness, 'I do not sleep when I am on duty.'

'Then why didn't you answer sooner? I've been ringing for over five minutes. I want you down here immediately.' He cut the connection.

He yawned, did up the top button of his shirt and tightened his tie. Ties were the invention of the devil. But it wasn't so easy to leave one off in winter as it was in summer when even dandies like the captain sometimes, in the privacy of their offices, went about open-necked.

He left and went down the back stairs and along the ill-lit corridor to the captain's office. There was a second man in the room whom he knew. 'Good afternoon, Doctor.'

The doctor stood up and shook hands.

Alvarez, his heavily-featured face looking rather sad, picked up a chair from the far wall and set this in front of the desk, next to the doctor's. He sat, well aware that the captain felt he should have waited until asked to sit.

'Doctor Palasi has come here to tell me that a wealthy Englishman died in La Huerta at eleven-fifteen this morning.'

They both stared at him as if they expected him to make some comment. But really he didn't care if a hundred wealthy Englishmen had died.

'Señor Freeman . . .' began Palasi.

The captain interrupted: he had the lean, nervous, thin-lipped face of a constant interrupter. 'At the beginning, the doctor thought it was cholera. But the tests showed that the cause of death was not cholera.'

They both stared at Alvarez again and this time he thought he ought to say something. 'So what was it, Doctor?'

'Only further tests will say for certain, but both the specialist and I became convinced that he died from the effects of a poison.' He scratched the side of his nose. 'What's more, we reckon the poison was from a llargsomi.'

'What's that?' asked the captain, who had not heard this part of the story before.

'A fungus, very similar in appearance to an esclatasang.'

'And what in the hell's that?' The captain was fast becoming annoyed because he was being made to appear ignorant.

The doctor showed his surprise. 'An esclatasang? Absolutely delicious! A plateful of those are fit for any king.'

'It's the Mallorquin name for an edible fungus which grows wild,' said Alvarez. 'You find it amongst old leaves under bushes and trees and in places like that.'

'Literally, it means popping blood in the sense that the pus in a boil pops out when you squeeze it,' said the doctor, who was a didactic man. 'The liquid in an esclatasang is red.'

'What a way to call something you eat!' said the captain, with disdainful scorn: like any Spaniard from beyond Catalonia, he had always regarded Mallorquin as a barbaric language and this merely confirmed his view.

'And this other thing, is it very poisonous?'

'Extremely. The main active principles are, of course, amanite and phalloidine, which are cytotoxins. As is common in fungi poisonings, if the symptoms show themselves within three hours the patient has a good chance of recovery; if they don't, he hasn't. Señor Freeman showed no symptoms for something like fourteen hours after eating on Thursday evening . . . I must, at this point, though, stress the fact that only the medical tests now being conducted will say for certain what the cause of death was.'

'It's good enough for me,' said the captain. 'We must findout whereabouts this llargsomi was picked and then search out and destroy all others there are.'

'Señor,' said Alvarez. 'I'm afraid that will not really be practicable. One can find the occasional llargsomi wherever esclatasangs grow and they grow all over the island.'

'If that's the case, how is it half the population hasn't been poisoned?'

'Every islander is taught the difference between the two almost from the time he starts walking. When you break a llargsomi, the liquid exuded is colourless. Also, flies never settle on them.'

'And so does everyone on this benighted island spend his time trying to see which fungi the flies avoid?'

'No Mallorquin with his wits about him would make a mistake, even if they do look so similar to someone who's ignorant of the difference,' said the doctor testily, annoyed by the slighting reference to Mallorca. 'There have been very few cases of poisoning by llargsomis in the past ten years.'

'Then how did this one happen?'

The doctor shrugged his shoulders.

'Obviously, we're going to have to make very careful enquiries. And perhaps we shall find that it isn't all that simple to tell the difference between them. I will question the cook exhaustively.'

'If I may suggest when you question her . . .' began Alvarez.

'You will accompany me.'

Alvarez gloomily stared at his shoes, which badly needed polishing.

The captain stood up and tugged a crease out of his uniform jacket. 'We will go right away, since this is a matter of great urgency. Doctor, you will hold yourself in readiness for any further consultation.'

'Naturally,' snapped the doctor, freshly annoyed by this unnecessary order.

They left the building together and then parted, the doctor going to his new Seat 131, the captain and Alvarez to the former's old Seat 124.

The captain drove with a careless disregard for other users of the road and Alvarez, always inclined to be nervous when being driven, closed his eyes and quietly asked St Christopher to look down with kindness on one poor sinner and protect him.

The captain lost his way, a fact which did not help his temper, and it was twenty minutes later before they drove through the gateway of Ca'n Ritat. The captain stopped with squealing brakes. 'Not bad. Not bad at all,' he said, as he stared at the house.

Alvarez looked at the soil and saw it was a rich dark brown and not very stony, so that it was not surprising that the garden was a mass of flowers and flowering shrubs. But soil that good ought to be growing vegetables, not flowers.

They had left the car and were walking towards the front door of the house, to the accompaniment of considerable barking from the dog, when Matilde stepped out of the kitchen into the courtyard. The captain turned into the courtyard. 'Are you the cook?' he asked curtly.

Disturbed because of his rank and frightened by his authoritative manner, she just nodded.

'What's your name?'

'Matilde Blanco, señor.'

'Right, I want a talk with you.' He looked past her and at the kitchen door. 'We'll go in there,' he said, striding forward.

Alvarez waited for Matilde and then he followed the other two inside. He looked around the kitchen and saw electric cooker, very large refrigerator, deep-freeze, washing-up machine, mixer, and rôtisserie, and he wondered how much it had cost to equip this kitchen. His mother had used only a charcoal fire and yet she had been the finest cook in the world.

'The English señor died this morning, almost certainly from eating a llargsomi,' said the captain abruptly, as if addressing a subordinate.

She stared at him. Her face was white and her eyes, reddened from past weeping, again filled with tears. 'It was terrible,' she murmured. 'Mother of God, he was in such pain.'

'Yes, yes, all very sad, but it's over and done with. What we have to discover now is how you came to cook him a llargsomi.'

'How I . . . señor, I never cooked him a llargsomi.'

'Don't be silly about this. He died from eating a poisonous fungus and you cooked his supper.'

'But I would never cook a llargsomi. And in any case . . .'

'The facts are too obvious, señora, to admit of weak excuses. You must have made a mistake.'

'Señor, I swear by all the holy saints . . .'

Alvarez interrupted her, speaking in an easy, friendly voice. 'Señora, we have to try to find out how the Englishman came to eat a llargsomi. We understand the señor ate the esclatasangs on Thursday evening and so we naturally thought you must have cooked his meal?'

She shook her head.

'Who did cook it, then?' he asked, with endless patience.

'He must have done, mustn't he?'

'Why?' snapped the captain.

She looked at him with renewed nervousness. 'But the esclatasangs were in the dish in the larder when I left the house on Thursday evening and they weren't in it the next morning. And there were the dirty plates for one person from the night before.'

'That's certainly straightforward,' said Alvarez. 'Señora, is your husband here at the moment?'

'No, señor, he is in Barcelona. His brother is very ill and perhaps is going to die so Luis had to go to him. You see, Antonio is younger and Luis had to look after him when his parents died during the war and so they are very close together.'

'I very much hope, señora, that your husband finds his brother is not as seriously ill as you have heard. Doctors can be very pessimistic if it is to help their reputations.'

'But when the señor died here . . . I thought, perhaps this is an omen.'

He firmly shook his head. 'An Englishman would never let himself become an omen for a Mallorquin. It would be beneath his dignity.'

'Enough wasting time,' snapped the captain. He smacked the palm of his hand down on the side of his immaculately creased trousers. 'There was a llargsomi amongst the esclatasangs.'

She shook her head.

'Don't be ridiculous, there must have been.'

'There can't have been, señor. Lopez brought them to me and . . .'

'Who's Lopez?'

She looked at him with fresh bewilderment.

He smacked his hands against his trousers again. 'Who is this Lopez who brought you the esclatasangs?'

'But everyone knows who he is, señor.'

'The saints preserve me,' said the captain. 'Listen, everyone does not know who this Lopez is. *I* do not know and I wish to know. Who is Lopez?'

She suddenly sat down, as if she could no longer stand.

'Perhaps he is the gardener?' suggested Alvarez, and he smiled at her encouragingly. She nodded.

'So the gardener picked the esclatasangs and gave them to you – is that what happened?' asked the captain.

'Yes, señor.'

'Why in the blazes couldn't you have said so at the beginning? So, now we know a little more. Then where is this gardener now?'

'But in the garden, señor.'

The captain had the sudden thought that she was trying to take the mickey out of him, but when he glared at her and saw the look of apprehension he was satisfied that she had not so dared. 'We'll go and speak to the gardener.' He turned smartly and strode out of the kitchen into the courtyard. The dog began to bark, hoping for some attention, but he marched past it without stopping.

'Don't you go on worrying,' said Alvarez to Matilde. 'It doesn't seem as if you've anything to blame yourself for.'

She was reassured by his words and also by the friendly expression on his square, heavy-set, dark-complexioned face which suggested some of the love he felt for most living things. 'I swear by the Holy Virgin, señor, that there was no llargsomi in the esclatasangs. Always, always, I check, even though it is Lopez who brings them. The señor couldn't have died from eating a llargsomi.'

'Maybe you're right and we'll discover it was really too much alcohol. The English like killing themselves off that way.'

He left the kitchen and went out into the courtyard. From his right he heard the sound of the captain's shouting. He walked out of the courtyard, pausing to pat the dog on its head, and then down a loose gravel path which wound past roses, geraniums, and chrysanthemums, to a shallow pond in which a number of goldfish swam lazily around and under water-lilies. The captain, red in the face, was shouting at Orozco. Alvarez was amused to see how this squat, solidly and stolidly featured man who was leaning on the handle of a rake, was staring into some private distance as if he were totally unconcerned with what was going on about him.

'I'm telling you, he died from eating a llargsomi,' shouted the captain.

Orozco briefly returned from his private distance. 'Impossible.'

'Don't bloody tell me it's impossible when I'm telling you it happened. He ate a llargsomi and it killed him. You picked it, mistaking it for an esclatasang.'

'Impossible.'

'Goddamn it, haven't I just said it happened?' The captain fingered the belt around his waist and it was possible to imagine he was wishing he wore a revolver. He glared at Alvarez, said, 'you talk to him and see if you can get any sense,' and stamped off, disappearing behind a low palm tree.

Orozco hawked and spat. Alvarez said in Mallorquin: 'He comes from San Sebastian. Up there, they all get like that. I suppose it's the climate.'

'Are you from this island?'

'Don't I sound like it?'

'Yeah.'

There was a shout from behind the palm tree. 'I'm going back to the post.'

Alvarez jerked his thumb. 'Always in a rush. As soon as

he gets to one place, he wants to be up and off to another.'

'Silly bugger,' said Orozco contemptuously.

'You've just about got him taped. He didn't even know what an esclatasang was! And when he heard the English señor had probably died from eating a llargsomi, he said we'd have to find every one on the island and root them up.'

Orozco guffawed.

'Then he wanted to know how anyone ever dared eat an esclatasang.'

'Why not give him a llargsomi to taste?'

The captain shouted out: 'Are you coming?'

'I reckon I'll stay on here a bit and walk back, señor,' Alvarez replied.

They heard the slam of a car door. The engine started, the car backed, turned, and accelerated down the drive, scattering loose gravel behind it.

Alvarez undid the knot of his tie and unbuttoned the collar of his shirt. He brought a pack of cigarettes from his pocket. 'D'you use these?'

Orozco took one and lit a match for them. 'It's good-looking soil you've got here,' said Alvarez. 'Must grow well?'

Orozco nodded.

'It's a pity you have to mess around with flowers and don't grow any vegetables.'

'Come,' said Orozco. He led the way past the fish pool, along the side of the swimming pool, the surface of which was attractively patterned with cloud reflections, and beyond the old donkey well which had been restored.

Alvarez stared at the rows of lettuces, cauliflowers, potatoes, beans, artichokes, and cabbages. 'I'm telling you, that's the finest showing I've seen for many a long day. And look at these cauliflowers – how d'you manage to get 'em this early?'

'D'you like 'em?'

'Love 'em.'

'Then I'll cut you one.' Orozco took a penknife from his pocket and, with the slow measured steps of a true country-man, walked along between the two rows of cauliflowers as he searched for the largest one. He finally bent down and cut one half-way along the row.

When it was handed to him, Alvarez shook his head in admiration. 'It's a real beauty.'

'He didn't like 'em.' Orozco jerked his head in the direction of the house. 'Said they was only fit for pigs.'

'He'll never know what he missed . . . Seems odd, doesn't it, that he died from eating a llargsomi? It's a long time since the last death like that which I can remember. Being a foreigner, of course, he wouldn't have known how to watch out . . . But I keep forgetting, you picked 'em, not him.'

'And what I picked was all esclatasangs.'

'It looks like there must have been a llargsomi among 'em.'

'I'm telling you, I picked all esclatasangs. D'you reckon I can't tell one from t'other?'

'But in that case, where could the llargsomi have come from?'

They were silent. A thrush flew past and Alvarez watched it circle a castor bush. He hoped it wouldn't be killed during the shooting season because he liked to see birds on the wing, not killed in the name of sport – not that he ever refused to eat a thrush if one, or preferably two, were offered to him. They were delicious. He heard a donkey bray and when that stopped there was the un-musical sound of a number of bells which were strung round the necks of either goats or sheep.

'What kind of a bloke was the señor?' asked Alvarez finally.

'A loud-mouthed ram.'
'Always after the women, was he?'
'If I've seen one brought here, I've seen a hundred.'
'Lucky man.'
'Silly bitches,' countered Orozco.

CHAPTER VII

Caroline saw that Mabel's car was parked outside Casa Elba so she paid the taxi-driver and added a small tip. The driver smiled his thanks and left.

She went along the side of the bungalow towards the front door. Only a narrow path through the maquis scrub had been cleared by the previous owner and Mabel had never bothered to have this enlarged or even kept trimmed so that now shrub branches reached out to worry passers-by. Mabel was as careless about the look of the outside of the bungalow as of the inside.

She opened the door. Her face was puffy and her eyes were reddened. Caroline did not have to ask if she had heard the news. 'I'm terribly, terribly sorry, Mabel.'

Mabel said nothing but stepped to one side and Caroline went in. The small kitchen was to the right, the passage to the bedrooms to the left, and the very large sitting-room straight ahead. It could have been an attractive, warm, friendly house if only Mabel had taken the trouble to make it so. A fire had been burning in the open grate along the north wall, but the logs had rolled apart some time ago and now were smouldering, giving off little or no heat but plenty of smoke which kept billowing into the room. On one of the small occasional tables was an opened bottle of brandy and a glass.

'Fenella told me what happened, Mabel, and she asked

me to say how sorry she is. She'd have come to tell you herself, but didn't want to upset you.' That was a lie – Fenella had never suggested calling for fear she'd become involved. But Caroline was ready to lie if it would help someone else if she did so.

Mabel stood by the sideboard which was against the dividing wall of the kitchen and she fiddled with a brass ornament. 'I . . . I never went to see him before he died.'

'Don't you think that's as well? I know people often do go out of a sense of duty, but when it's a really serious illness and you can't help at all, surely it's better to stay away and remember the person as you last saw him, fit and well?'

'Don't you know how I last saw him?' she demanded wildly.

Caroline was shocked by the effect her words had had.

'Hasn't anyone told you? That's a change for this place where that kind of news usually gets around in a flash because it's all so hilarious.'

She was hysterical and needed a sedative, thought Caroline.

'I went to his place on Thursday because I thought that was when he'd asked me to lunch.' Mabel walked over to the table with the brandy on it and picked up the bottle. 'I swear I thought he said Thursday.' She poured out a drink, drank, looked across the room at Caroline and then walked towards the kitchen.

'I don't want anything, thanks,' said Caroline.

Mabel ignored her and went into the kitchen, to return with a glass into which she poured a generous brandy. Then she crossed to a wooden chest from which she brought out a siphon. She added soda to the brandy before handing Caroline the glass. 'I'd been looking forward so much to having lunch with him.'

How could she so have failed to come to terms with life

and herself? wondered Caroline. How could anyone so lumpy and awkward, so ill-equipped for romance, have remained as unthinkingly romantic as any schoolgirl?

'I didn't know so I went straight in because the front door was ajar. Well, we often do that out here, don't we? We don't always knock and wait. He'd got a friend, a woman. She . . .' Mabel drank, finishing the brandy. She put the glass down. 'They were . . .' She poured herself another brandy. 'She was naked and her hands . . . Oh God, it was terrible! I felt sick. And all he did was tell me I'd got the day wrong.'

Life dealt her only jokers, thought Caroline. Or did she deal them to herself?

'He kept on and on telling me it was all my fault because I'd got the day wrong.'

'I suppose that really was to try and hide his embarrassment.'

'But he didn't apologize. Not once. And the woman was laughing at me.'

That seemed very unlikely, in the circumstances.

'It doesn't matter what happened, though, I ought to have gone and seen him when he was ill. But I didn't know he was so ill that he was dying.' Tears suddenly spilled down her cheeks. 'You've got to realize, I didn't know he was dying.'

Caroline met Anson at the back bar which overlooked the square in Puerto Llueso. He was dressed in dirty, paint-stained sweater, jeans, odd socks, and plimsolls.

He studied her face and saw the lines of worry and said: 'What the hell's up, Carrie? Are you in trouble?'

'Nothing's the matter with me, but a lot's wrong with Mabel. I went to see her earlier and can't stop thinking about her.'

Anson crossed to the bar and ordered a coffee and a

brandy, returned to the table with the brandy. He cradled
the glass in his hand. 'Stop worrying so hard about other
people, Carrie. You can't carry everybody's troubles on
your shoulders.'

'She was in such a state.'

'She's never in anything else.'

'You might be a bit more sympathetic,' she said indig-
nantly.

He shrugged his shoulders. 'How can you sympathize
with someone who never ever gets anything right? Look at
her finding Geoffrey with some woman. She not only gets
the day she's invited totally wrong, she just barges into
the house without waiting to see if she's welcome. Anyone
but her knows that Geoffrey spends more time horizontal
than vertical.'

'You can't blame her for going inside. The front door
was open and she was so certain she'd been invited for
Thursday.'

'An ounce of common sense would have told her to ring
the bell and wait to see if he was occupied.'

'I think that's being silly.'

'Realistic.'

'Just because you can't stand her . . .'

'Listen, Carrie, I don't actively dislike her, but between
us there just aren't any smoke signals. And I'm not talking
like I am just because I don't get on with her. There was a
woman in the village back home just like her. She fell down
the stairs in her house three times before she finally fell a
fourth time and broke her neck.'

'So what does that prove?'

'That this woman was mighty clumsy.'

The barman called out and Anson stood up and went
over to the bar and collected the coffee. Caroline un-
wrapped the two cubes of sugar and dropped them into
the cup. 'I tried to get her to let me stay the night with her

because she was in such a state.'

'If you're not careful, you'll be nominated for a saint-hood.'

'Stop jeering,' she said, with sudden anger.

'Not jeering, just laughing. And if I couldn't laugh at trouble, I'd've cut my throat years ago.'

She stared up at him and thought that he would always fight back by laughing. But what lay behind that laugh? A compassion which life had taught him could come too expensively, or an indifference towards other people's troubles? She could never be quite sure.

'Carrie, you've done ten times as much for her as anyone else in this place, so stop worrying. And just remember something when you're in danger of getting too upset. It's always possible that Mabel likes to be kicked around by life.'

'What a damnfool thing to say! You know what she thought of Geoffrey. She's absolutely beside herself with grief.'

'But she must have realized what kind of bloke he was. And how he'd chase after anything under twenty-five which wore a skirt. So why did she keep after him unless she liked to be hurt?'

'I don't think I like you very much tonight. Something's happened to you, hasn't it? Something not very nice. Has Ramón laid down a deadline for you becoming a partner?'

He finished his brandy. 'Carrie, you still have the capacity to amaze me. Who'd imagine that someone so far removed from the more sordid aspects of life would be able to pinpoint them so accurately?' He looked at his glass, then very casually reached down to his trouser pocket to feel how much money he had left. 'The next round's on me,' she said. He swore silently as he shook his head, but when she looked at him he picked up the glass and went over to the bar.

'What did Ramón say?' she asked, as he sat down again.

'He wants to expand, he wants a partner who can really work and deal with the English-speaking tourists or residents, and he wants both in a hurry so he can plan for the next season. Can I or can't I find the million and a half? ... Very soon, I told him. Not to worry. But he's a good Mallorquin and won't believe a word until he's got the pesetas in his hand.'

'You must let me lend you the half million so that you can persuade a bank to give you the rest.'

'I told you, forget the idea.'

'But it's ridiculous for you to sit back on your pride ...'

'You force me to further confessions ... Despite my previous high-minded refusal of your money, I crept round to two of the local banks and put the proposition to the managers: I find half a million, you lend me a million. Nothing would give us greater pleasure, honoured customer ... I'll swear there were tears in their eyes. But money is so very short. All business is difficult and so have I a little security? Say a million pesetas' worth? I'd have flogged it a long time ago, wouldn't I? I told 'em. So very sorry, honoured customer. We'd so have liked to help you ... Always very polite, you see.'

'Then maybe a third bank will help, or if not, a fourth. There must be one manager around with imagination.'

'I doubt it: imagination isn't a banking characteristic.' He smiled sardonically, mocking himself. 'In any case, I was only stringing them along. I'd never really borrow that half million from you.'

'Not even when it's the one chance you've always longed for?'

His expression momentarily hardened.

CHAPTER VIII

Alvarez awoke, remembered it was a Sunday, and relaxed. How to spend the day? If it was fine, a drive up into the mountains where there were no tourists and there remained space and solitude? . . . But, of course! He'd promised to take the two children along to one of the beaches so that they could fly the new kite. He smiled. Children completed a home. If Juana-Maria had lived they would have filled their house with children and then through them they would have lived after death. Perhaps a little of him would live on through his cousin's two children, even if she wasn't really a cousin and his relationship to them had become too remote to be readily explained.

He remembered the cauliflower from Ca'n Ritat. He experienced the fierce longing to own land which so often gripped him. One day he would buy some and grow cauliflowers even larger and denser-headed than the one he had been given. Perhaps if he stopped drinking and buying so many presents for the children he could save enough money. But children ought to be given toys and when he drank brandy he could forget Juana-Maria for a little while.

He climbed out of bed, crossed to the window, opened it, and pushed back the shutters. It was a sunny day, warmer than expected because the wind was coming in from the south. He stared over the roofs of the houses, their tiles forming a mosaic of soft pinky-browns, at the hermitage and church on Puig Antonia, now looked after by nuns, and he wondered whether Santa Antonia would listen to his plea to own a little land? He wasn't certain how a saint saw worldly ambitions, yet felt that his ambition was surely one of which he need not really be ashamed.

Downstairs, his nephew, Juan, was reading a comic. 'Hullo, Uncle. You promised to take us to the beach today.'

'I haven't forgotten,' said Alvarez, scrumpling Juan's already untidy hair.

'Mother said you would probably forget because you'd drunk so much coñac when you said you'd take us.'

'I am very fond of your mother, but sometimes she does tend to exaggerate. Report back to her that you are quite definitely going to the beach this afternoon.'

'Why not let's go this morning? After lunch you'll sleep and snore and it's getting dark so early now.'

He sighed. 'All right. But you'd better understand that I'm making a very great sacrifice on your behalf.'

'You mean you won't be able to go boozing at the club?'

'The young of today are far too smart for their own good.'

Juan laughed and at that moment the telephone rang. 'It'll be for your mother,' said Alvarez hopefully.

He was wrong. 'The Institute of Forensic Anatomy has rung through, Enrique,' said the Guard. 'The English señor died from eating a poisonous fungus called *Amanita Mallorquinas*.'

'I suppose that means it was a llargsomi?'

'I wouldn't know about that. Superior Chief Salas says that you're to investigate very carefully how the Englishman came to eat a poisonous fungus and to take whatever steps are necessary to see it doesn't happen again.'

'Well, it won't happen again to him, will it? . . . Why in the hell is Salas getting in on the act?'

'The captain rang him to make a full report because it is a matter of public urgency.'

'The captain's a stupid bastard.'

Juan laughed and Alvarez looked at him through the opened doorway and shook his fist, daring him to tell his mother what he had said.

'I'm not arguing with you over that, Enrique . . . Have a happy working Sunday.'

Alvarez replaced the receiver. If the captain had minded his own business, nothing need have been done until tomorrow. But thanks to that interfering idiot, he was now going to have to spend Sunday trying to discover how an Englishman could have eaten a llargsomi when Orozco and Matilde swore blind that in the kitchen there had been only esclatasangs.

He crossed the sitting-room and went through into the kitchen. 'Juan, that was a call telling me I've got to work today. So the trip to the beach is off unless I can wrap up everything before the afternoon.'

After breakfast he drove into the square, which for the morning was ringed by 'No Entry' signs, and parked by the steps.

The raised part of the square was a mass of people and stalls selling all the vegetables in season, and some imported from the Peninsula or the Canary Islands which were out of season, nuts, cheese, eggs, dried herbs, and bedding-out plants. He pushed his way through the crowd to the church, against the wall of which was a barrow selling sweets. He chose several packets of the more sickly-looking kind which he knew his nephew and niece liked, then walked past the café – this one was patronized far more by the locals than the one on the south-east side of the square – and along to a toy shop where he spent quite a long time deciding which two toys to buy. That done, he returned to the Club Llueso and had two brandies.

He drove out of town and along the Puerto road to the islands and there cut up past the new football ground to the camino and Ca'n Ritat.

Matilde was in the kitchen, washing down the tiled floor which was spotless. She was clearly glad to have someone to talk to and she offered him a coffee.

He sat at the table set close to the far wall and while she made the coffee he stared at all the electrical equipment and wondered what it could do that an efficient wife couldn't. And what happened when there was a power cut?

She poured out two large cupfuls of coffee and put one in front of him, together with milk in a plastic bottle and sugar in a bowl. 'I can't get used to it,' she said, as she sat. 'I mean, not having to get his breakfast and find out what he wants for lunch and all that sort of thing.'

'Have you any idea what's going to happen here?'

She shook her head.

'Are you sorry this job will come to an end?'

She pursed her lips. 'Luis will be. But I didn't like the way the señor entertained.'

'Because it made your work so hard?'

'Not that. Hard work's never worried me.'

'Then it was all the women he had along?'

'That's right.'

'It must have been upsetting for someone like you, señora, but the English have very different standards from us.'

'How can women behave like that? And some of them were even married!' She spoke with genuine amazement. She knew only virtuous women who honoured their marriages.

He stirred sugar into his coffee and drank. 'Did he ever have his family along: you know, parents, brothers, and sisters?'

'Never once, not all the time we worked here.'

'Which is how long?'

'Just about three years.'

The English seemed to take their family ties about as seriously as their marriage vows. 'All in all, would you have called it a good job?'

'I suppose it wasn't too bad. We had Monday afternoon and evenings off and one week-end in four. And if one or other of us wanted an extra day, he usually gave it to us unless he was in a mood. You could find worse jobs and that's a fact. Except for all the women. He was a . . . But he's dead now, God rest his soul.'

'Perhaps He will. I was once told that the English God is very generous . . . Look, we've heard today that he definitely died from eating a llargsomi and I've been ordered to find out how it happened. You must have thought about things a lot since yesterday. Are you quite sure you didn't make a mistake and let a llargsomi through?' He motioned with his hand. 'Don't get anything wrong. No one's going to clap you in jail because you made a mistake. It can happen anytime, to anyone.'

'There was no llargsomi among the esclatasangs,' she said forcefully. 'Señor, I am not a stupid fool. So every time Lopez picks and brings me esclatasangs, which the señor liked so much, I checked every one to make certain there was no llargsomi, even though Lopez would never pick one by mistake.' She leaned forward, her expression becoming still more earnest. 'Señor, I am of this island even though I came from the other end. Could any islander handle esclatasangs and not check that there were no llargsomis among them?'

'Perhaps there are times, though, when one is not quite so careful because one is in a great hurry, or has a very bad headache . . .'

'I am not lazy, I did not hurry, I did not have a headache. I tell you, there was no llargsomi.'

'But if not, how did the señor come to eat one and die?'

'I do not know. Perhaps God, to punish his wickedness, changed an esclatasang into a llargsomi.'

It was a fascinating idea, but one which Alvarez regretfully thought unlikely. 'I'll have to find something definite to tell my superior chief, but so far all I've learned is that it couldn't have happened.' He stood up. 'Is Orozco, the gardener, here today?'

'He has all the Sundays off.' She spoke shortly.

He smiled at her. 'I believe you absolutely, señora. But my superior chief comes from Madrid and he will believe no one without complete proof, not even himself . . . Thanks for the coffee.' He went out of the kitchen into the courtyard and she followed him. The dog which had been lying down in the sun in front of its kennel stood up, barked twice, and hopefully wagged its tail. 'What's his name?' asked Alvarez.

'Cheetah. He was abandoned and when Luis found him his ribs were almost out of the skin. Luis said he should be killed, but I said no, I would make him well. So now look at him! As fat as a pig that's ready for a matanzas.'

Alvarez crossed the courtyard and patted the dog's head and fondled his ears. A car came along the dirt track, turned into the drive and then braked to a stop in front of the courtyard. 'It is the señorita,' said Matilde in a low voice. 'She came here on Thursday and saw the señor . . .' She stopped.

He watched an ungainly woman, a plastic bag in her hand, climb out and come round the bonnet. 'What did she see the señor doing?'

'I cannot say it.'

Caroline got out of the near side and as she stood upright Alvarez stared at her and he fell in love.

Mabel came forward, walking hesitantly. 'Hullo, Matilde,' she said in a low voice. 'I've brought some scraps for Cheetah.' The dog might have understood her because it began to pant and its tail wagged furiously. Mabel opened the bag and spilled the contents on to the flagstones and the dog ate with noisy gusto.

It wasn't her looks, thought Alvarez with bewilderment, although she was as beautiful as an orange grove at blossom time. It wasn't that she promised that ripe, earthy experience which twisted a man's soul – she didn't. It was because there was an air of simple goodness about her which reminded him with aching intensity of Juana-Maria.

'When I saw those scraps were left . . .' Mabel stopped, then resumed speaking very hurriedly. 'It would have been such a shame to waste them . . . So I thought . . .' She suddenly sneezed several times.

Caroline spoke lightly, trying to lessen the air of emotion which Mabel had introduced. 'You're quite right, Mabel, he really does eat like a vacuum cleaner.'

Matilde, who understood more English than she spoke, said: 'I feed him good, señorita.'

'I can see you look after him really well,' said Caroline quickly. She smiled at Matilde. 'He's in wonderful condition. It's just that some dogs always eat very quickly, even when they've only just had a meal. Cheetah is obviously one of those.'

She'd gone out of her way not to hurt Matilde's feelings by making it clear that they didn't believe that the dog wasn't being fed properly, thought Alvarez, yet most English wouldn't give a damn about what a Mallorquin maid thought. Juana-Maria had always been thinking about other people's feelings.

'We'd better go,' said Mabel. 'I only wanted to come . . .' She stopped, clearly far too embarrassed, even ashamed, to continue.

'Yes, of course.' Caroline smiled at Matilde and Alvarez. 'Goodbye, then. I do hope we didn't disturb you too much.' She turned and walked to the car and this had the effect of making Mabel do the same. A moment later, they drove off.

'She's a very silly woman,' said Matilde scornfully.

'What d'you mean?' snapped Alvarez, before he realized he was in danger of making a fool of himself.

Matilde stared at him in sudden apprehension.

'I am very sorry, señora, I was talking to myself about something entirely different . . . Now, then, tell me why you think that woman is so silly.'

She looked doubtfully at him, but was quickly reassured by his expression. 'She was in love with the señor. A woman like her. He just laughed at her. Especially after what happened on Thursday when she saw him . . .'

'Saw him what?'

'I cannot say. But he had another woman here.'

'The other señorita who was here just now?'

'No. I have never seen her before.'

He was furious with himself for daring to think such a thing could ever have been possible. 'D'you know who this first woman was?'

'No, señor. But when he said she was coming to lunch he called her Veronica and said she was on holiday and he wanted to show her what the island was really like. As if it wasn't obvious what he really wanted! . . . He said to put out the cold meat then to keep out of the way. I am a decent woman, but even so I know what such orders mean. So I put out the meal and told him and returned to the kitchen. I heard a car arrive and it was the juice-less señorita who has just been. She went into the house and soon she began to shout at him and when she came out crying I knew what she must have seen.'

CHAPTER IX

Alvarez stood at the bar and stared at the mirror. He saw a middle-aged man with lined, coarsely featured face, whose eyes were bloodshot and whose hair was beginning to thin. You simple fool, he said to his reflection. You, a failure, a peasant without a single *cuarterada* of land to call his own, old enough to be her father . . . But her golden image continued to dance in his mind.

'Give me another,' he said.

The barman picked up his glass. 'You look as if you'd lost a few thousand-peseta notes.'

'There are worse things to lose than them.'

'Don't bother to tell me what they are . . . Do you really want another coñac?'

'Didn't I ask for one?'

'All right, all right, keep your hair on.'

When he had looked at her he had seen the quiet moon in the star-studded sky, the sparkling of still seas, the distant mountains framed against a sunset sky. And when she had looked at him, what had she seen? An ugly, time-scarred peasant . . .

'Here you are, Enrique. Drink it up and for the love of God cheer up or you'll frighten any other customers away.'

He emptied the glass, but he didn't cheer up.

On Monday morning Alvarez drove to the small unreformed finca which lay beyond Ca'n Ritat. Here time had almost, if not quite, been defeated and the small-holding was pretty well self-sufficient. The family kept a mule for working the land, a cow for milk and calves, and pigs, sheep, goats, rabbits, chickens, guinea pigs, and pigeons, for eating. They fed the mule on straw, dried field beans, and grass, the cow on grass, straw, and ground algarrobas, the pig on dried figs and anything else that was left over, the sheep and goats were left to graze among the scrub land but were sometimes given some dried field beans, the chickens and pigeons had wheat, barley, or oat tailings, the guinea pigs and rabbits lived on grass. The family grew corn and handed much of it to the miller who gave them tokens which they exchanged at the baker for loaves. They grew three crops each year and after the tomato harvest there were always long strings of air-dried tomatoes everywhere. They harvested the olives, with six-metre bamboos and had them pressed and the oil came green and pungent. They trod their own grapes and made a red wine that was filled with lees. They netted small migratory birds, or caught them with worm-baited snap-traps or on branches covered with bird-lime, and they ate these with a simple pleasure untroubled by any ecological thoughts.

The house was small and hunched-looking. Most windows had no glass, only solid wooden shutters. In heavy rain the roof leaked in several places. There was no bathroom, only a cold tap in the kitchen. The privy was outside the back door. But as if to prove that time must always gain at least a foothold, there was electricity and in the sitting-room a large, much chromed television set.

The couple looked old, but he guessed their ages at not much more than his own – life had been hard, though not without its compensations. On the battered desk in the sitting-room were photographs of two daughters, as babies, as girls at their first communion, and as brides.

'A coñac, señor?' said the man, obviously nervous about having a policeman in his home.

'I could really do with one,' he said.

They bustled about, getting in each other's way as they

searched for the bottle of brandy and a clean, unchipped glass. Finally, the man poured out nearly a tumblerful of brandy for Alvarez.

'Your health,' said Alvarez. 'And may your crops strain tight the granary doors.'

They began to relax as they appreciated that he was of their kind. He talked to them about mules, the problems of maintaining the fertility of the soil when this was constantly being leached out, and the damage mole-crickets could do to a crop when the moon was in the first quarter. Finally, he led the conversation round to Ca'n Ritat.

'He never used to talk to the likes of us,' said the man and his wife nodded agreement. He did not say this deferentially or complainingly, merely as a statement of fact. He had a natural pride in himself, his family, and his work, and it would never have occurred to him that he might have considered himself socially inferior.

'I've been told he was fond of entertaining the ladies?'

The man laughed with Rabelaisian gusto. 'If I'd a ram as active as him, I'd have a flock a hundred strong. Where'd he get 'em all from, that's what I want to know. They weren't around like that when I was a young 'un.'

'Not that you could have done anything about it,' said the woman.

The man winked at Alvarez. 'Here, is that right he ate a llargsomi? Couldn't the silly bastard tell the difference from an esclatasang?'

'It seems he couldn't.'

'Matilde says they was all esclatasangs,' said the woman. 'There weren't no llargsomis among 'em.'

They stared at Alvarez with sharp interest. He shrugged his shoulders as if it were a matter of no consequence. 'He must have picked up one from somewhere . . . D'you see him at all on Thursday?'

They thought back. After a while, the man said: 'Seems like it could be Thursday he turned up at the house after merienda with a woman. Skirt was so short there's no knowing why she bothered to wear one.'

'You shouldn't have looked,' said his wife.

He laughed shrilly. 'If wild asparagus grows in the lane, d'you think I'm going to walk past it?' He rubbed his unshaven chin. 'What d'you say that big car of his cost?'

Alvarez had not seen Freeman's car, but he guessed it was an expensive one because Freeman had obviously been a man who believed in show. 'Maybe as much as a million.'

They thought about that, but it was really beyond their comprehension that anyone could be so wealthy that he could waste a million pesetas on a car.

'Did you see him in the afternoon or the evening on Thursday?'

The man shook his head. The woman said: 'The dog was barking and howling.'

'It is always barking and howling,' said the man. 'The inspector's not interested in that.'

'But perhaps I am,' said Alvarez, 'because I need to know about everything unusual. What kind of time was this?'

'It were dark,' said the woman, as if that covered everything.

'Soon after dark, or later on?'

The man spoke testily. 'I tell you, that dog were always kicking up a row.'

'Not like it was then,' she corrected him. She spoke slyly. 'Perhaps Lopez had kicked it.'

'Belt up,' he said, his voice angry.

It was obvious to Alvarez that the woman wanted to tell him something and yet either hadn't the courage to come right out with it or else, like so many peasants, seldom approached a subject directly. 'Lopez is the gardener, isn't he? I'm surprised you think he might kick the dog: I'd have thought he was a different kind of a bloke to that. And come to that, are you certain he was around the place at that time? Did you see him?'

'When it was dark?' asked the man scornfully.

Alvarez looked a little put out, as if this was something he had overlooked. 'You might have heard his voice and so known he was there.'

'We heard him earlier on, that's for sure,' she said. Her husband glared at her, but she took care not to look in his direction.

With infinite patience, Alvarez discovered what it was she wanted to tell him. As far as they knew, Orozco had left before dark as he always did. But before he left, and while it was still fully light, she had been out picking beans and had heard Freeman having a row with Orozco. 'The English señor was always shouting at Lopez,' said the husband. With obvious reluctance she had to admit that this was so.

She still had something to tell him. 'Was it,' suggested Alvarez, 'a worse row than usual?'

' 'Course not,' said her husband, interrupting what she had been going to say. 'Anyway, Lopez don't say nothing much but lets the señor go on and on.'

She leaned forward and lowered her voice. 'Maybe you don't know? He fought for the other side!'

Alvarez stared at her, surprise stretching his face. So this was the big secret. Forty-odd years ago, Orozco had fought for the Republicans and this fact was still held against him.

'I said right from the beginning we should've told the English señor. But he – ' she jerked her thumb at her husband – 'he said it didn't matter because an English señor wouldn't understand. Is that right?'

'I wouldn't know,' he answered disinterestedly.

She was disappointed and scornful that he couldn't appreciate the importance of what she had just told him.

Alvarez, conforming to etiquette, put down his glass with a little brandy left in the bottom. He stood up. 'Thanks a lot for all your help.'

The man nodded. The woman stared at him, puzzled that a man of so little intelligence should be in the police.

CHAPTER X

When Alvarez entered the Guardia post, the duty corporal told him that Superior Chief Salas most urgently wanted to speak to him.

He telephoned Palma. Superior Chief Salas asked many questions and made many suggestions. Where had the poisonous llargsomi come from? Had the dead man eaten it through negligence and, if so, the negligence of whom? If the gardener swore he had picked no llargsomi and the cook swore there had not been one among the esclatasangs which had been cooked by the dead man, where could it have come from? Could anyone reasonably continue to view the death as purely accidental? Had the inspector bothered to investigate whether there were any motives for murder? He had? Superior Chief Salas sounded surprised. There had been some sort of row with the gardener? And a very painful scene involving a woman who had been in love with the dead man? These facts must be investigated thoroughly. What was the row about? The woman who interrupted and the woman who was interrupted must be interviewed. And had it, by some chance, crossed the inspector's mind that it would be a good idea to investigate the Englishman's financial affairs? And where the nearest llargsomis grew? And who . . . ?

Sweet Mary, Alvarez thought gloomily, why did life have to get so dreadfully complicated?

The bank manager was small and sharp and he dressed very smartly in a well-pressed suit and a shirt with a semi-stiff collar. He put his elbows on the desk, joined the tips of his fingers together, and rested his chin on his fingers. 'He was very well off, but I don't think I can tell you anything more than that. When I spoke to him it was only about business.'

'Did his money come from England?'

The manager lifted his chin, parted his fingers, and lowered his hands. He made all movements with such preciseness that often they appeared rather affected. He opened a folder. 'I can't answer that question, Inspector. Whenever it was necessary, Señor Freeman paid into his account a sum in pesetas.'

'Just pesetas?'

'That's right.'

'Isn't that a bit odd? Most foreigners must surely cash foreign cheques or pay in foreign currency?'

'In banking, Inspector, it is a truism to say that nothing is unusual. Other countries have currency regulations which foreigners who reside or visit here are at great pains to circumvent. My job is to provide such people with banking facilities provided there is no contravention of Spanish law.'

'Are you saying that because Señor Freeman paid pesetas into his account he was probably fiddling his money through to Spain?'

The manager spoke with strong disapproval. 'The word "fiddling" is not one I care to hear used in this context.'

'But if you couldn't care less how foreign money reaches you, why shouldn't he bring in the foreign currency? Where did all the pesetas come from?'

'I have no idea.'

'You don't think that perhaps he was fiddling Spanish currency?'

'Good God, no!' said the manager, shocked by the thought.

Normally, Alvarez loved the Port and Llueso Bay, as yet relatively unspoilt by tourism, but after tramping around to visit hotels and pensions for what seemed like hours he was so tired that he not only sat down at one of the front bars, he then had not the energy to enjoy the view. His misery became complete when he was handed the bill for one small brandy.

He left the bar and walked along the pavement, past shops many of which were shut for the winter, to the Hotel Llueso which, like many other hotels, had been enlarged during the great tourist boom and was now in some difficulty because of the minor recession. The black-coated receptionist studied his ill-fitting, creased clothes and the frayed collar of his shirt and his manner became supercilious. 'Yes?'

'Cuerpo General de Policia,' snapped Alvarez, with satisfaction.

The receptionist became obsequiously polite. 'I'm so sorry, I didn't realize. What can I do to help? Do you wish to see the manager?'

'All I want to know is if you have an Englishwoman staying here whose Christian name is Veronica.'

'And her surname is?'

'I haven't the faintest idea.'

'Oh, dear! It will be most difficult to try to discover just from a Christian name . . .'

'Then the sooner you get started, the better. In the meantime, I wouldn't refuse a coffee.'

He went into the lounge and happily relaxed in a comfortable armchair and was peacefully drifting off to sleep when a waiter brought him a large pot of coffee, milk, sugar, cup, saucer, and spoon, on a silver tray. He poured out a cupful of coffee and added a dash of milk. He had just lit a cigarette when the receptionist hurried into the lounge.

'I have found that we do have a señorita with the name of Veronica. She is Veronica Milton.'

'Have you her passport?'

'Yes, señor. It is here.'

Alvarez opened the passport and looked at the photograph. 'It obviously could be her. See if she's in the hotel.'

'If there's some sort of trouble . . .'

'I'll tell you about it all in good time.'

He helped himself to a second cup of coffee and was just stubbing out a second cigarette when a woman came into the room. He studied her. She was younger than she had looked in the passport photo and far riper. He stood up and shook hands. 'Señorita Milton, I am Inspector Alvarez. Thank you for coming here to speak to me.'

'But what's the matter? Why d'you want me? What have I done wrong?' Her voice became high as she remembered the Guardia with sub-machine guns she had seen on her arrival.

'Señorita, please don't disturb yourself, I assure you there is no need for that. Though I perhaps have to give you some bad news . . . Do sit down.'

'Is it my family?' she asked, as she sat. 'Has Mum . . .?'

'There is no bad news from England, señorita. The bad news concerns a person who lives here, on this island. I think you may know him. Señor Geoffrey Freeman.'

'Geoff! What's he been up to now?' Her voice became sulky.

'I fear he has died.'

'He's what?'

'Clearly, you had not heard this?'

'Of course I hadn't. Why, on Thursday he was alive and . . . What happened? Was it an accident?'

'Señorita, Señor Freeman died from eating a poisonous fungus and now it is my job to try to understand his life for the past few days. I think you saw him on Thursday and so perhaps you will tell me how you first met him and then what happened.'

'I . . . I'd rather not.'

'Please understand, it is very confidential with me.'

'But . . .' She fiddled with a strand of hair just above her ear. 'I suppose . . .' She shrugged her shoulders. 'It was like this. I was having a drink with Di – she's my friend – at one of the cafés and he walks along and sits at the next table and gets chatting. You know how it goes, don't you? People talk to strangers easier out here than they do at home.'

'Of course, señorita.'

'Well, we got friendly and he said how about going to Palma for the day and having lunch at some wonderful restaurant he knew. Di was friendly with a bloke she'd met at the hotel so she wasn't too keen, but I . . . I thought it'd be a bit of a lark. He picked me up in his car on Thursday and I asked him which restaurant we were going to and he said no restaurant but back to his place for lunch where his cook had prepared everything. So we went to his place.' She sighed. 'It's a lovely house.'

'Indeed it is, señorita.'

'With that swimming pool and all the flowers. My dad would've loved to see it . . . You haven't got a fag I could borrow, have you?'

'I am so sorry. Please have one of these.' He offered her a pack. 'I fear they are black tobacco.'

'Blue, black, or red, I just need a fag. Geoff dead!' When she'd lit the cigarette from the match he'd struck, she inhaled greedily.

'Did you have a pleasant lunch at his lovely house?'

'You've just got to be joking! He was hungry, all right, but it wasn't food he was after.'

'Perhaps you could explain?'

'Well, it's all rather embarrassing . . . I mean, I don't want you to think . . . Look, he mixed the gins too strong.'

'Too strong for what, señorita?'

'Too strong for me to remember that a girl's best friend are crossed legs.'

'He tried to make love to you?'

'There was no holding him.'

'And you and he . . .?'

'It was all his fault – I mean what happened, not that we . . . Oh hell! It's complicated. Look, I said to him, let's go upstairs. I mean, if it's going to happen a lady wants it to happen in privacy. But he said he'd told the cook to keep out so no one would bother us. The nerve of him, making all the arrangements before I'd arrived!'

'So you were where in his home?'

'In the sitting-room. We had some drinks – too much gin for me – and then he got fresh and before I knew what was happening, I was . . . Well, I wasn't as I'd started, if you understand. Then this old faggot comes shrieking in.'

'Old faggot?'

'I don't know who she was, do I? Looked like my Great Aunt Ida, the one whose husband gassed himself. She shouted her head off that he'd asked her to lunch, he said he'd told her to come on Friday . . . Went on and on arguing like that and there was me, in a state of complete . . . I'll tell you, I was in a complete state.'

'And do you think she was upset?'

'Upset? She looked like she was going to have a fit. And I'll swear she'd have chucked something at me if there'd been anything handy and if she hadn't been so busy trying to tell him he'd said Thursday. Then she began sneezing like her head was coming off and she cleared out.'

'And what about you, señorita?'

'You can imagine how I felt! I've never been so embarrassed in all my life. I had said let's go upstairs, after all.'

'You make it sound as if he was not embarrassed?'

'Honest, I don't know what you'd have to do to embarrass him. Cool! There he was, caught in the act as you might say, but did that worry him? All he wanted was to get cracking again as if nothing had happened. I told him, I'd had enough. I wanted back to the hotel.'

'How did he react to that?'

'Got annoyed, but that was just too bad. I mean, one needs to be in the mood. And after being interrupted by that old faggot, I plain wasn't in the mood.'

'Did he cook you a meal before he brought you back here?'

'Are you having me on?'

'I don't think so, señorita, although I am not quite certain what you mean by that.'

'After being embarrassed silly, d'you think I was worrying about lunch? Even when I got back here, I couldn't eat, I was so upset. I'm not used to having people behave like him.'

You could have fooled me, thought Alvarez.

Orozco was transplanting late variety cauliflower plants, working with a slow, ponderous rhythm, when Alvarez arrived. He'd heard the car brake to a halt in front of the courtyard, the three short barks of the dog, and the crunch of feet on gravel, but he didn't stop, nor did he look to see who had called.

Alvarez reached where he was working. 'D'you use plenty of dung? They say pig dung's the best for cauli-flowers, horse for cabbages. I reckon there's not much difference if you rot it down well.'

Orozco picked up a plant, used the mattock to fold open the soil, dropped the plant into the hole and butted the earth with the heel of his boot. 'Dung's dung.'

'D'you feel like taking a breather?'

Orozco said nothing, but set out the remaining plants. Then he straightened up, pressed his fists into the small of his back, and stretched. The sunlight picked out his face to show it as rough, stubborn, and proud.

Alvarez offered a pack of cigarettes. 'Is there somewhere we can go and sit down?'

'Feeling tired, are you?'

'And old.'

Orozco looked briefly at him, then said: 'Come on.'

Alvarez followed along a gravel path which led past orange trees whose fruit was showing the first flush of gold to the drive. They turned into the courtyard and crossed this to one of the downstairs rooms below the servants' quarters on the north side. Clearly, the room was the garden store: there were tools on the walls and on shelves, heavy-duty grass-cutter, pots, wide gauge hose-pipe, and a workbench littered with hand tools, broken pots, and empty seed packets. Orozco sat down on one of the two old wooden chairs.

'I hear you and Señor Freeman didn't always get on too well together?' said Alvarez, as he sat.

Orozco reached over to the workbench and picked up a penknife and a square of wood which had been roughly shaped yet whose final form was not yet readily identifiable. He squinted at the wood and then carefully began to slice off thin slithers of wood from one side.

'Seems like there were often rows?'

He held the wood out at arm's length and studied it.

'What did you mostly row about?'

'The garden.' He resumed working on the wood.

'In what way?'

'In all ways.'

'Then what exactly was the trouble last Thursday afternoon?'

Orozco said uninterestedly: 'He was on again about what happened to all the seeds he gave me.'

'What did happen to them?'

'They didn't grow.'

'Why not?'

'Because I never planted 'em.' He looked up and spoke contemptuously. 'Think I'm fool enough to waste me time with foreign seeds?'

'Had he discovered you hadn't planted 'em?'

'Him? He'd never discover anything unless it wore a skirt. He just got to shouting because I said them seeds wasn't no good.' He spoke with sly satisfaction.

'Why did he get quite so upset?'

'Reckoned nothing shouldn't ever go wrong for the likes of him.'

'Wasn't there anything else upsetting him?'

'No.'

'Doesn't seem much to row about.'

'Tell him that, not me.'

'I take your point.' Alvarez stared at the grass-cutter. After a while he stood up and crossed over to study it. 'Looks man enough for near any job.' He rolled the machine back along the floor to gauge its weight. 'I hear you fought for the other side. Why? This island was for the Nationalists.'

'I was young and stupid enough to think that ideas mattered.'

'D'you see much fighting?' Alvarez left the machine and returned to his chair.

'A bellyful.'

'How d'you make out? Did you get wounded at all?'

'Twice.'

'D'you feel afterwards it was worth it?' he asked with companionable curiosity.

Orozco sliced off a couple of chips of wood, then suddenly spoke more freely. 'A young bloke gets ideas and fights for 'em because there's no one to tell him different or he won't listen if there is. And when the bullets and shells are thicker'n fleas on a hedgehog and his belly's turned to water, he gets to discover that all his ideas along with all the ideas of everyone else what's fighting are a load of balls. The only things what really matter in life are a hole to shelter in, water to drink, grub to eat, and friends.'

'So what did you do when it was all over?'

'In the end, I got back to this island.'

Alvarez wondered what odyssey of hardships was concealed behind those laconic words. 'Did Señor Freeman know about all this? Did he go for you, jeering at you for being a commie?'

'You think a great hidalgo like him worries about what an ignorant peon like me has ever done or been?'

'It's odd who can worry about such things.'

'Only people who never actually held a gun and shot or got shot at.'

'What about Luis?'

'He fought.'

'On which side?'

'He was bright. He chose the winning side.'

'The only recipe for success.' Alvarez folded his arms

across his chest and stared down at the floor. After a while, he said: 'I don't know how we got to talking about the war. I'm supposed to be finding out how the señor came to eat a llargsomi.'

Orozco changed his grip on the knife and, applying pressure with his thumb, very carefully shaved off a slither of wood.

'You must have thought about things. How d'you reckon it happened?'

He didn't answer.

'Señora Blanco says there was no llargsomi among the esclatasangs you gave her.'

'Of course there bloody wasn't.'

'Yet the señor died from eating one. It had to come from somewhere.'

'Maybe he picked some more for himself and made a mistake.'

'Why should he have picked any more?'

'Who knows what about an English señor?'

'Where did you go picking esclatasangs?'

'There's some rough land beyond the urbanizacion. They grow there. Else I look up the Laraix valley.'

'And there are llargsomis as well?'

'Have you ever picked esclatasangs when there weren't?'

'Never. Did you see any when you picked the last lot?'

'Yeah. And I kicked 'em to bits.'

CHAPTER XI

'Well?' demanded Superior Chief Salas over the telephone.

'Señor,' answered Alvarez, 'since you rang this morning

I have been making very extensive enquiries . . .'

'With what results? Was it murder or was it an accident through negligence?'

'Señor, at the moment it is impossible to be certain . . .'

'It is your job to be certain. Have you been in touch with England to see if they can help?'

'Not yet, because . . .'

'Perhaps because it has not occurred to you that a man's background might be of importance? Inspector, I hope you don't make quite so many mistakes in this case as you did in a previous one when for a long while you totally misidentified the man who had died.'

'That was rather a complicated case . . .'

'I imagine that you must find every case highly complicated.' He rang off.

On Tuesday morning, Alvarez set the alarm for six o'clock and when it sounded he forced himself to get out of bed straight away. He dressed and went down to the kitchen where he warmed up some soup. He was about to drink this when Dolores, wearing a flowered dressing-gown over her nightdress, entered.

'What in the world are you doing up at this time, Enrique? Is something wrong?'

'It's just that I'm going to pick some esclatasangs and if I don't start as soon as it's light enough someone else will strip the land clear.'

She frowned. 'You're getting up early just to pick esclatasangs?' She was a strikingly handsome woman, with an oval face and jet black hair.

'Why not, when we all like them?' He switched off the gas and poured the soup into a bowl.

'Because usually not even an earthquake will get you out of bed until the last possible moment.' She shook her head, asked him if he'd like some chorizo fried, and then brought out from the larder a chorizo from which she cut several slices. She fried three in oil and he ate them with pan Mallorquin.

After breakfast he went out to his car, which proved to be in one of its more temperamental moods and only started at the seventh attempt, and drove out of Llueso on the bridge over the torrente, only a trickle since there had not yet been heavy rains up in the mountains, crossed the Laraix road, and continued along the lane which wound through the dark brown, fertile soil of the Huerta until he reached a dirt track leading off to the right, along which he parked.

The ground here was sloped – the mountain immediately to his left began to rise steeply only half a kilometre from where he was – and he was able to look out over the land below him and pick out the roof of Ca'n Ritat. From there to where he stood would take an active man no more than five minutes, he judged.

He began his search. It was a very rocky area, with boulders up to two metres high, and among the typical maquis scrub grew pine, evergreen oak, and an occasional algarroba tree. He used a stick to scratch through the rotting leaves on the ground, especially close to bushes, and in half an hour he had found over three-quarters of a kilo of esclatasangs, one or two of them as big as six centimetres in diameter. He had also found two llargsomis. He studied the two varieties of fungi, perhaps for the first time truly mystified by the fact that one was delicious to eat and the other deadly. Why? The esclatasang, resembling a chanterelle, was fawny-brown on top, to a certain degree tulip-shaped, with a rippled surface: underneath it was grey-brown with complicated gills: draw a thumb across it and a red liquid oozed out: leave the picked fungus for a time and green veining would appear. The llargsomi at a cursory glance hardly differed in appearance: the colouring and the shape seemed the same. But a closer, more searching inspection showed that the tulip shape was more pronounced and the surface was more unevenly rippled, the gills were more grey than brown, and when the surface was disturbed the liquid exuded was colourless.

He drove back to the house and handed the esclatasangs to Dolores. He watched her take them out of the plastic bag and visually check each one, even though she must have had every confidence in his ability to distinguish what was safe from what was deadly. No Mallorquin, certainly no adult Mallorquin, could or would ever accidentally cook a poisonous llargsomi.

Caroline turned off the front road on to the western arm of the harbour and drove past the landing-stage for the Parelona ferries and the restaurant to the boatyard. She parked by the main gates, which were roughly opposite the point at which the harbour arm began to curve, and climbed out, becoming aware of the continuous slap-slap of halyards against masts, a sound peculiar to any mooring.

She went through into the yard and saw Anson on the hard, painting anti-fouling paint on to the keel of a yacht in a cradle. She threaded her way past piles of chocks, old oil drums, and tackle. He climbed down off the wooden box on which he'd been standing. 'What's brought you here at this time of day, Carrie? Nothing wrong, I hope?'

'Nothing. Just a piece of news for you.' She managed to sound casual.

He relaxed and then, perversely, perhaps because he had instinctively braced himself for bad news, said rather shortly: 'Couldn't it have waited? I've got to get this job finished today.'

'Stop behaving like a grumpy bear and take enough time off to come and have a coffee with me. I'll bet you haven't had a break all day?'

He hesitated a moment, then jumped down. 'OK. But I can't be long.'

She laughed. 'No one's ever going to accuse you of being obsequiously polite.'

In the past, he had found the world too hard a place for him ever to be bothered with politenesses, but when he was with her he often cursed himself for his seeming crudity which came from embarrassment as much as ignorance or lack of experience.

They left the boatyard and walked past the yachts, each one of which he studied with a professionally critical eye, to the road and then down to the bar overlooking the square. It was almost empty and the barman greeted them warmly and asked Caroline, in Spanish, how she was. Anson said she was fine and ordered two coffees, then led her over to one of the tables. He was suspicious of any man who smiled at her.

He brought out a pack of Ducados cigarettes and offered one. 'What's the news that simply couldn't wait?'

She stared at his strong face, which could look almost harsh at times, and she wondered how she was going to persuade him to forgo his pride. 'Teddy, before I tell you, will you promise me something?'

'What?'

'First promise.'

'All right. Now what have I promised?'

'That you won't get angry with me.'

He smiled. 'OK. But I can belt you one without getting angry.'

She laughed, because despite his hard, quick temper it was impossible to imagine that he would ever hit her. 'I just couldn't stop thinking how awful it was that you'd been offered the chance of a lifetime and yet you couldn't grab it with both hands on your own and wouldn't accept any help.'

'I've tried to explain why . . .'

'Don't worry, I got the message,' she said, with light mockery. 'You are a man of inflexible principles and concrete will-power . . . With emphasis on the concrete.'

'What's made you so chirpy?'

'Teddy . . . I think I've done it!'

'Done what, for Pete's sake?'

'Persuaded Mabel to lend you the money so that you can become a partner. Think what it means! That new sign will go up outside the yard. Mena and Anson. And in a couple of years' time you'll be building the future winner of the America's Cup.'

He said nothing.

'I'm so excited I feel as if I'd just won the lottery.'

'I thought she reckoned I was a beach-bum who needs to be packed off to darkest Scotland to work in the salt mines?'

The barman brought the coffees to their table.

'I suppose it's a horrible thing to say, Teddy, but poor Geoffrey's death does seem to have changed things for the better. I've done what I could for Mabel, trying to cheer her up, and this morning she suddenly started saying how wonderful I'd been to her and how I was the only person on the island who cared anything for her . . . I tried to tell her how wrong she was. Everyone's sorry for her.'

'How do you manage to see through such thick rose-tinted spectacles? Carrie, the only thing that really upsets most people out here is when the price of gin or brandy goes up.'

She ignored his cynical comment. 'And then she told me that because I'd been so kind she wanted to do something for me and what could she do? I'm afraid I rather seized the opportunity and went on again about you and the wonderful chance you'd been offered, but couldn't take. She thought for a bit, with that odd look of hers, and then said that if I liked you enough to go on trying to help you, you must be a different kind of a person from what she had always thought and so if that's what I really wanted she'd like to help you if she could. Teddy, if you'll talk things over with her, I think you'll find she's ready to lend you most or all of the money you need to buy the partnership.'

'Why should she do that for someone she so dislikes?'

'Heavens above, I've just explained!'

'People don't change their character that far. Haven't you ever been told about the leopards?'

'Teddy . . . You're looking at things from all the wrong angles. What she wants to do is something that'll give me pleasure.'

'It sounds screwy.'

Her excitement had been so great that now her disappointment was equally intense. 'Oh, Teddy. I thought it would be so wonderful for you.'

'You've got to stop being naïve about people. The old girl's had a nasty shock because she was stupid enough to go for Geoffrey. You've given her a shoulder to cry on and so she's temporarily filled with Christian thoughts, but in a couple of days she'll have recovered and reverted to her normal, bitchy self.'

'That's being beastly.'

'Carrie, the world isn't made of sugar and spice. It's made of rats and snails and puppy dogs' tails.'

'Only when people think it is . . . Why assume that Mabel didn't really mean what she said? Why be so certain she'll go back on her word? Suppose she's like I know she is and not like you think she is? Then she really does mean everything. Teddy, you've got to come and see her and talk over your plans.'

'And bow down in front of her and knock my forehead
on the floor?'

'Don't be such a fool,' she said sharply. 'Start swallowing this stupid pride of yours which for some ridiculous
reason makes you turn on anyone who tries to help you.
Why can't you find a bit of humility and learn to accept
help when it's offered?'

It was not a question he had ever asked himself.

Alvarez sat at his desk and wondered how Dolores would
cook the esclatasangs. In oil, with garlic and parsley, so
that they melted in one's mouth? The telephone rang.

'There's a Telex message just in from England, Inspector. I'll read it out . . . "Reference Geoffrey Freeman,
previous address in UK given as twenty-one, The Rise,
Larkton, passport number five four three nine six nine.
Regret address non-existent, passport stolen, name of
Geoffrey Freeman unknown" . . . Well, that's it, Inspector.'

'Thanks a million.'

'Always ready to help a colleague.'

CHAPTER XII

'Alvarez,' said Superior Chief Salas over the telephone,
'did you not assure me that this case was perfectly straightforward and the identity of the dead man was beyond
question?'

'I don't think I ever put it quite in those terms,
Señor . . .'

'Not so many months ago you reported dead a man
who was alive. Now you report dead a man who never

existed. What will it be next time?'

'Señor, it was your suggestion I should ask England for information. It is they, not me, who now say the Englishman never existed.'

'A ridiculous argument. I've no doubt that what's actually happened is that you've sent the wrong information.'

'I gave them the details from his residencia and I have been back on to the office and they assure me that I got all the details right.'

'Find out who he really was and try to decide once and for all whether he was murdered.' Superior Chief Salas slammed down the receiver.

The English, thought Alvarez, were the world's trouble-makers, even when dead. He stood up, yawned, looked at his watch to see how long it was before he could break off for lunch, sighed, and left the room. His car was parked in the square and he walked to it. He drove out on to the Puerto Llueso road and then, at the islands, went past the new football ground and up to the urbanizacion. He took the spur road down to Casa Elba.

Señorita Cannon interested him because he was certain she had no counterpart in Spain. There were ungainly women, ugly women, even, it was said, sexless women in Spain, but all of them would possess dignity and pride. Señorita Cannon could have neither dignity nor pride.

When she opened the front door, she said: 'What do you want?' in a tone of voice devoid of all welcoming hospitality.

'Señorita, I would be most grateful if you would be so kind as to answer one or two questions for me.'

With obvious reluctance, she stepped to one side to let him enter. Lying about the sitting-room were papers and magazines, records in their jackets, two bottles in the grate which had not been cleared of ash, and a clothes-

horse in front of the fireplace on which were several under-
clothes. Dolores, he thought, would have to be very
seriously ill before she ever allowed her home to get in
such a state.

'What do you want to know, then?' she demanded
roughly. As she finished speaking, a telephone rang in one
of the bedrooms along the corridor. Without bothering to
apologize, she swung round and left to hurry down the
corridor.

He crossed the room and looked at the records. They
all seemed to be of old, romantic musicals in which
everyone nice lived happily ever afterwards. Poor
woman, he thought with sudden compassion. She could
only know romance vicariously. He moved and looked at
the books in the large bookcase, expecting them all to be
romances. A few obviously were, but the rest of the titles
showed that he'd been wrong in attributing to her such
narrow intellectual and emotional interests. On the
shelves were books on archaeology, history, travel,
biographies, flora, fauna, and insects of Northern Europe
and the Mediterranean . . . and a green bound book en-
titled *Vegetable Poisons* by P. J. Meegan.

It was not a very thick book. Each chapter was clearly
headed: the poppy; hashish; cocaine; atropine, hyoscya-
mine, and scopolamine: curare; the double-faced stroph-
anthus and the two hemlocks: the death cap, the destroy-
ing angel, the fool's mushroom, and the edible table top
. . . The chapter on poisonous fungi had obviously been
well read and two pages, facing, were quite dirty. Almost
at the bottom of the first of these was a fresh paragraph
which carried on to the second page:

There grows in the Balearics, and in particular on the
largest of the islands, Majorca, an edible fungus known
locally as esclatasang. (In Mallorquin, a dialect of
Catalan, one of the four languages spoken in Spain,

this means popping blood. The esclatasang exudes a
red liquid.) These are held to be delicious and are
highly priced – perhaps too highly priced for anyone
who has eaten the field or oyster mushroom in northern
Europe. The casual fungicologist, however, eager to
sample the specialities of the islands, must be on his
guard when searching for these fungi. For among the
esclatasangs may be found occasional examples of
Amanita mallorquinas, distinguishable by the savant, but
not by the incognoscente. *Amanita mallorquinas* (known
locally as llargsomi – in Mallorquin, this is a corruption
of llarg somni, 'long sleep'; the Mallorquins often
display a macabrely ironic sense of humour) like its
cousin *Amanita phalloides*, must be considered quite
deadly. A small amount if eaten will cause severe illness, a whole cap will almost invariably cause death
which comes in its most distressing form, racking the
body with acute abdominal pains, very severe vomiting, raging colics . . .

He heard her returning along the corridor. He replaced
the book in the bookcase.

When she entered, she looked at him with surprise, as
if she had forgotten he was there, and then flopped down
in one of the armchairs.

'Señorita, I will be as brief as I can be,' he assured her
kindly.

She continued to stare at the fireplace.

'Certain points concerning the unfortunate death of
Señor Freeman have raised questions.' He walked over to
the second armchair and sat down. 'It occurs to me that
you may be able to help answer the questions. How long
did you know Señor Freeman?'

She might not have heard him.

'Señorita, how long did you know Señor Freeman? Did

you know him before you came to this island?'

'Why d'you say that?' she demanded shrilly. 'I never met him before. D'you hear – I never met him before.'

Alvarez rubbed his heavy chin. 'Then it is only coincidence that you and Señor Freeman applied for your first permissions and then your residencias on exactly the same dates?'

'Yes.'

'Perhaps you should know that I have been told you were friendly with the señor from the time you first came to Llueso.'

'Who's been prying into my life?'

'Señorita, in a small community surely everything is known to everybody?'

'No.'

He waited, because he thought she was going to say something more, but she was silent. 'Señorita, may I see your passport, please?'

'Why d'you want to see it? I won't show it to you.'

'I am very sorry, but I must insist on seeing it.'

She stared with hatred at him for a while, then she jerked herself out of the chair and left the room. When she returned, she threw the passport at him.

He studed the number. 'Señorita, would it again be only coincidence that the number of your passport is in sequence with that of Señor Freeman's?'

'Oh God, why can't you leave me alone?'

'You did know him before you came to this island, didn't you?'

She closed her eyes as if to shut out the threatening world.

Because he was a man of compassion, he hated the necessity of having to question her further. 'Señorita, do you remember my asking you whether you knew about the poisonous fungus which on this island we call llargsomi and I now learn the experts call *Amanita mallorquinas*?'

She shook her head.

'You told me you had never heard of it. Yet there is a book on the shelf over there which describes the llargsomi and details very closely what happens to a person who eats one.'

'I've never read that.'

'But the pages are much used . . . Señorita, poison does not always strike as a book says it will. One person is killed by an amount the book says is merely dangerous: another person can eat an amount that is said to be fatal and live. Tell me, did you just wish to make him ill, to suffer a little for what he had done to you?'

She opened her eyes and stared at him.

'On Thursday you went to his house and found him with another woman. It would have shocked anyone, but perhaps it shocked you more greatly because you were very fond of the señor. So you determined to punish him a little . . .'

'Are you trying to say I gave him the poison and killed him?'

'I do not think you intended him to die . . .'

'You filthy swine! Get out.' She jumped to her feet. Her face was twisted with hatred and her mouth was opening and shutting as if she were panting for air.

'Señorita . . .'

She screamed. She leaned over and picked up an occasional table and threw it. Her aim was poor and the table missed Alvarez by at least a metre. It hit the settee and fell to the ground. She began to sneeze, violently, and tears, caused either by the sneezing or her wild emotions, flooded down her cheeks. Her nose dripped.

Sweet Mary, he prayed, see me safely out of this madwoman's house. He came to his feet and hurried across to the front door, coward enough to imagine her finding a handy carving knife and racing towards his unprotected back . . .

He pulled open the door, shot out, and slammed the door shut behind himself. What ignorant fool, he wondered, had described the English as a phlegmatic race?

As he walked towards his car, parked under the shadow of a crooked pine tree, another car came down the slip road. He identified the driver as the woman he had first seen in company with Señorita Cannon and he experienced another, and very different, rush of emotion.

Caroline braked the hired Seat 600 to a stop, opened the driving door and climbed out. 'Hullo,' she said. 'We met the other day, didn't we? You're a policeman. Have you just been in to see Mabel?'

He was momentarily tongue-tied. The passenger came round the bonnet and Alvarez looked at him for the first time. He saw a man in his early twenties, powerfully built, with a strongly featured, tanned face, dressed in very worn yachting T-shirt, jeans, and plimsolls. A boat-bum, he thought immediately, having seen so many of them hanging around the harbour, scrounging what they could, working only when they had to. He knew a sharp, indignant anger. That she should be in the company of such a man.

'What's up, then?' asked Anson, not intending to sound as belligerent as he undoubtedly did.

Alvarez continued to stare at him.

'Seems like he doesn't speak English. Come on, Carrie, let's go in and get it over with.'

'I speak a very little, señor, but that little not very well,' said Alvarez, with the self-deprecating politeness which in Spain sometimes took the place of rudeness. 'I fear I make many mistakes.'

'Well, it sounds to me as if you speak it wonderfully

well,' she said gaily. 'I only wish I could speak Spanish half as well.'

Her eyes were deep blue where Juana-Maria's had been dark brown, yet to look into them was to look at what had lain in Juana-Maria's.

'How is Mabel?' asked Caroline. 'I hope she's a bit better. She's been so depressed that I've been worried.'

'Señorita, I am afraid that now she is also disturbed by what I have said to her.'

'That's all we bloody wanted,' muttered Anson.

'Don't get into a panic, Teddy,' said Caroline.

'Who's panicking?'

'From the sound of things, you are. Look, if she's too upset now for us to talk to her about it all, we'll just come back some other time.'

'Señorita,' said Alvarez, 'permit me to suggest that it would be best not to speak to the señorita on this occasion. She is not as calm as one would wish.'

'Then that's that, isn't it!' Anson kicked a stone across the road. 'I told you it would be a waste of time.'

She spoke to Alvarez. 'Have you any idea why she's so upset?'

'I had to ask several questions, señorita, and she did not welcome them.'

'Questions about Geoffrey Freeman's death?'

'That is so.'

'Oh, Lord, no wonder you say she's disturbed! Teddy, it's not going to be the slightest use speaking to her to-day.'

'There's not much time left,' he said perversely.

She wanted to tell him to snap out of it, but realized that he was on edge, suffering from excitement, apprehension, and reaction.

'Goodbye, señorita,' said Alvarez. When she smiled at him, he was momentarily a rich man.

He remembered her goodbye smile all the way to Llueso.

Alvarez was far too much of a countryman really to like any town, but he was never sorry to visit Palma because there was something rather countrified about those parts of it which weren't entirely dedicated to the tourist trade – also, the toy shops had a much greater selection than those in Llueso or Puerto Llueso and he could be certain of buying something really nice for his nephew and niece.

He drove into the underground car-park in the Plaza Mayor and walked round to a tapas bar where he had small dishes of squid, tripe, and meatballs, and a glass of wine followed by a brandy. From there he walked to the large toy shop in Calle General Mola where he spent over half an hour choosing two toys and it was not until well over an hour after arriving in Palma that he entered the Calle Juan Rives branch of the Banco de Credito Balear.

The assistant manager saw him in the manager's office.

'We've been handling an account in the name of Señor Geoffrey Freeman, Inspector, so when the request for information came through we immediately got in touch with you. I hope there's nothing wrong?'

Bankers always worried so, thought Alvarez. 'Nothing likely to upset you, I'd say. It's just that the señor has died and I need to know what sort of business you did for him.'

'That's easily explained. He has an account with us into which he occasionally pays large sums of money and on which he draws fairly regularly.'

'Was the money paid in with English cheques or bank drafts?'

The assistant manager looked annoyed at himself for not having the answer pat. He opened a folder and quickly read through some papers. 'All payments appear to have been made in Swiss francs by means of cheques.' He looked up. 'With most currencies having been so volatile, he's been fortunate to have been in Swiss francs.'

'Can you give me the name of the Swiss bank on which the cheques were drawn?'

'I don't think so. The cheques go to Madrid and then back to the issuing bank. Since no cheque was ever refused, I have no separate knowledge of which bank it was.'

'I wonder why he did things this way? It surely would have been easier to have worked entirely through you or his other bank?'

The assistant manager smiled with discreet amusement at such naïve questions.

'Is there anything more about his account you can tell me?'

'I don't think so, Inspector.'

'Then I've just one more question. Do you by any chance handle another account for an English señorita by the name of Mabel Cannon?'

'One moment. I'll make enquiries.'

The assistant manager left. Alvarez stared at the far wall and wondered whether if he were wealthy, with many millions of pesetas, he would appear less than middle-aged to a young woman with corn-coloured hair and deep blue eyes who lived in a world filled with evil and yet remained untouched by it.

The assistant manager returned. 'Yes, we do handle her account.' He tapped two sheets of paper he carried in his left hand. 'It's precisely the same pattern. Large sums of money paid in in Swiss francs, smaller sums in cash drawn out at roughly regular intervals. The only real difference is that the señorita has never withdrawn a very large sum since the beginning, when I imagine she bought her house.'

'How's that?'

'The most that's been paid in is around a hundred thousand and almost all withdrawals are for less than twenty thousand. But the señor paid in and drew out fifteen million.'

Alvarez whistled. 'When was this?'

'The middle of April . . . A man can do a lot on fifteen million, can't he, even in these days of inflation?'

Alvarez pushed aside the empty glass down on the desk and looked at his watch. Surely it was now too late to visit an English señorita who, despite appearances, probably worried about her virginity from the moment it became dark? An unwelcome shaft of honesty made him admit that he was afraid. What if she should be even more emotionally upset than on his previous visit? Would he escape with his life? He poured himself out another brandy and wondered why he couldn't reconcile himself to being a coward?

He drove from the Guardia post to Casa Elba. There were lights on inside. He sighed, because until now it had always been possible she might have gone out.

He left the car and walked, the uncut bushes brushing him, to the front door. He pressed the illuminated bell push and heard the bell sound.

She opened the door to the extent of the chain and peered out and when she recognized him her expression became bitterly antagonistic. 'What do you want now?'

'Señorita, I fear I have returned to ask you further questions.'

She said something he didn't catch, shut the door until she could release the chain, then opened it. He stepped into the house. There was a smell of cooking, but it was a thin smell, not the kind of rich, full, garlicky smell to which he was accustomed. Thank God he wasn't eating here! The sitting-room was in an even more untidy condition than previously and the record-player was playing a sugary waltz.

'If you've come to make any more filthy accusations . . ' she began aggressively.

'Señorita,' he cut in hastily, 'I am here to make no accusations, merely to ask you about a bank account.'

She stared at him for a few seconds, her head thrust forward, then she whirled round and strode over to a chair and sat.

'Señorita, you have a bank account with the Credito Balear in Calle Juan Rives in Palma.' He raised his voice to counter the music.

'Still spying,' she said contemptuously.

'I fear I have to make many enquiries when people do not tell me the full facts.'

'I've told you over and over . . .' She stopped abruptly and reached up to her throat. She had some difficulty with swallowing and after a while she stood up and clumped past him to go into the kitchen.

Through the open hatchway, between the sitting-room and the kitchen, he watched her fill a glass from the tap and drink. She waited, shook her head as if something were sorely puzzling her, and poured out another half glassful of water.

When she returned, there seemed to be a certain uneasiness to all her movements, as if something had suddenly begun to ache. She stared in front of her and ran her fingers through her mouse-coloured, straggly hair, trying to brush it away from her forehead.

'Señorita, you pay into your account with the Credito Balear certain sums of money in Swiss francs. Will you please tell me the name of your Swiss bank?'

She made no answer.

'I am afraid I have the power to make you tell me . . .' He stopped because she was plainly not listening to him and now there was a look of growing fright on her face as if she could see something of immeasurable evil.

'Señorita, what is the matter?'

She spoke croakily.' My mouth . . . It's burning.'

'Let me get you something to drink.'

She jumped to her feet and ran back into the kitchen and by the time he had reached the door she had poured out a third glassful of water. She drank with such desperate eagerness that water spilled over the edge of the glass and down the side of her mouth. Then, with only a split second's warning, she vomited.

Sweet Mother of Jesus, he thought, as the record ended with a sweep of violins, she's been poisoned.

CHAPTER XIII

The doctor, a small man with wide-apart, gentle eyes which were contradicted by a sharp nose and pugnacious mouth, said: 'She died at eight-fifteen this morning.' He looked tired and he spoke with the bitterness of a man who had fought to the extent of his skill and yet still lost.

Alvarez looked across the consulting room. 'She was poisoned?'

'I'm sure the answer's yes, but obviously no one will know for certain until after the post mortem.'

'Do you think it was a llargsomi?'

The doctor began to tap the desk with his fingers. 'I doubt it. I am remembering your original description of the way she had difficulty in swallowing and how she kept saying her mouth was burning. These are not the normal symptoms of phalloidine poisoning.'

'Then can you suggest what it might have been?'

'No. You'll have to wait for the reports.'

'It must have been strong to have acted so quickly?'

'Quick is always a relative term, isn't it? For her, death must have seemed unmercifully tardy.' His rate of tapping increased. 'I've seldom seen such suffering and been so powerless to ameliorate it.'

Alvarez shivered.

Bertha Jarmine was known as Bertha the Bitch (although it happened only twice a year to a bitch) and because she was so contemptuous of all standards, even those few which pertained around Llueso, she was disliked and feared by other women. She was said to be as hard as nails and in support of this was told the story of how the day after her second husband died she had given a cocktail-party to six of her strongest admirers to decide who among them would keep her bed warm that night. In fact, she had been seeking solace, not sex. What people failed to understand was that she was both wanton and faithful, self-centred and sympathetic, mean and generous. She might have thought of Caroline with the ridicule that the so-called fallen reserve for the so-called chaste and upright, but she honoured genuine goodness in others as much as she dishonoured the goodness in herself.

She drove, in her battered Ford which was on English plates and which she kept without paying the new tax, to Caroline's flat which was in a block set in an area of the Port which had managed to combine all that was worst in Spanish tourist development.

Caroline opened the front door. 'Hullo, Bertha. Come on in. What fun to see you . . .' She stopped because of the expression on Bertha's face.

Bertha went in. 'I'm sorry, Carrie,' she said, her words crisp but her tone sympathetic, 'but Mabel died this morning.'

Caroline, always affected by death and still more

affected by Mabel's because Mabel had died as awk-wardly and ingloriously as she had lived, began to cry. Bertha put her arm around her and led her into the sitting-room where, being a practical woman, she poured out a large brandy for each of them.

'But . . . but what was it?' asked Caroline. 'It was so terribly sudden.'

'The word's going round that she was poisoned,' replied Bertha. Caroline must inevitably hear the rumour before very long, therefore there was no point in trying to shield her from it.

'No one would poison her. Not Mabel. Why should anyone?'

'God knows.' She opened her handbag – typically, it was very large and of superb quality crocodile skin, yet she treated it as if it were plastic – and brought out a slim gold cigarette case. 'D'you want one?' When Caroline shook her head, she lit one. 'Did you see her at all yester-day?'

'I went to her home with Teddy on Wednesday, but the detective had just been talking to her and he said she was very upset. We didn't go in because I thought that if she was so upset it was best to keep away for a bit . . . If only I'd gone yesterday as I thought of going.'

'It wouldn't have changed anything,' said Bertha decisively. 'Did Teddy find her calmed down when he saw her?'

'But I've just told you, Teddy was with me and we didn't go in.'

'I'm talking about yesterday.' Bertha looked at Caroline with a sharp enquiry which was edged with sadness.

'Teddy didn't see her yesterday. He and I were going back there today.'

'Maybe it wasn't him who went to her place, then. You know how people out here always get everything mixed up and twisted round.'

'He can't have gone there. Why are people so beastly...'

'Look, Carrie, I know you carry his banner high. But you've got to realize he's not everyone's cup of tea. And if he did see her yesterday, you can't expect people . . .'

'I expect them to say the worst they can because they don't like him. And you know why? They know he was born the wrong side of the railway tracks. Why the hell don't they start realizing that the time's now, not fifty years ago? They'd have to change their attitudes fast enough if they went back to England.'

'You're not becoming over-fond of him, are you?'

'What's that to do with anyone else?'

'It's everything to do with you. He could hurt you pretty hard: he's that kind of a person.'

'If you can say that, you don't know anything about him.'

'I know his type well enough. What he wants, he grabs, and to hell with the consequences. I'd hate to see you get hurt.'

'I can look after myself.'

Bertha shook her head.

Alvarez looked at the telephone on his desk for several minutes before he finally lifted the receiver, dialled HQ Palma, and asked to speak to Superior Chief Salas. The secretary with the very refined voice said he'd have to wait because Señor Salas was very busy. While he waited, Alvarez pulled open the bottom right-hand drawer of his desk.

'Well?' said Salas rudely, not bothering with any preliminary greeting. 'Have you at last uncovered the true identity of the dead man?'

'No, señor. What's more, there has been a further small complication.'

'What's that?'

'You may remember I previously mentioned the name of Señorita Cannon, an English lady?'

'Of course. You told me you had every reason to believe she was responsible for poisoning the dead man. Have you arrested her?'

'No, señor.'

'Why not?'

'She has just died. I fear she had almost certainly been poisoned.'

There was a short pause before Superior Chief Salas spoke. 'Inspector, I must congratulate you! Although I had imagined that experience had left me incapable of being truly surprised by the course of any investigation undertaken by you, you have just managed to astonish me. Would it be too much to ask . . .'

Alvarez reached down for the bottle of brandy.

Alvarez put the key into the front door of Casa Elba and turned it. He pushed open the door and stepped inside. In the gloom, the ghost of the dead señorita chilled him and his ears were assailed by phantom shrieks . . . Sweet Jesus, he prayed, when death comes for me, let it come in kinder guise.

He crossed to the windows, opened them, and pushed back the shutters. The daylight, although not very strong because it was a cloudy day, banished the ghost. He went over to the desk and pulled down the flap. Because she had been so careless about appearances, he had expected to find the interior of the desk in total disorder, but instead there were folders neatly stacked, several bills clipped together, and an account book right up to date. The files were carefully labelled, in copper-plate writing: 'Current Mail', 'Copies', 'Bank Statements', 'Will'

'House', 'Car', 'Spanish Documents', 'English Documents'.

The will, in Spanish, had been drawn up by a local solicitor. Originally, everything she owned was left to Geoffrey Freeman. Then a codicil divided her estate between Caroline Durrel and Geoffrey Freeman, with the survivor taking everything. And separate from the will was a copy document, in French, which covered most of a large sheet of paper and at the bottom of which was provision for three signatures although there was no indication of whose these were to be. He tried, but failed, to make out what this was about.

He wondered what her estate was? There presumably was the house and its contents, but how much capital? He opened the folder marked 'Bank Statement'. Where the statements were not up-to-date, she had noted down all deposits and withdrawals and had kept running totals. There were 46,370 pesetas in the Banco de Credito Balear and 18,116 in the local bank. And on a plain sheet of paper, in her handwriting, she had noted the fact that there were 919,220 Swiss francs now standing to her credit in the Banque de Foch, in Zurich.

Nine hundred and nineteen thousand! How many pesetas to the Swiss franc? There were several papers strewn over the settee and he checked through them and found the local paper in English which gave the rate of exchange as just over twenty-seven . . . Over twenty-four million! He looked round at the untidy room with its tatty furniture and visualized the dead woman in her badly fitting clothes. Who in his wildest dreams would ever have imagined that she was worth over twenty-four million . . .?

Caroline Durrel was going to be very wealthy . . .

He checked through the rest of her papers and discovered that there was among them not a single reference to her life before she had come to the island.

Alvarez sent a Telex message to England. He gave details of Mabel's passport, a detailed physical description of her, the date of her arrival on the island and English address as supplied in her application for a residencia, explained that evidence suggested she was in some way connected with 'Geoffrey Freeman' who had died six days previously, and added that the señorita had the sum of over 919,000 Swiss francs on deposit in Switzerland. Could the police give him any information about her?

CHAPTER XIV

In contrast to Friday, Saturday was a day of warmth and sunshine and the land once more became beautiful and the mountains attractive, not lowering presences.

The Telex message arrived at eleven-fifteen in the morning. England reported that the address given did not exist, nor could they trace a Mabel Cannon. Further enquiries were being made.

Alvarez looked at the telephone on his desk. But there surely were times when things shouldn't be rushed and therefore to report to Superior Chief Salas now must be unwise?

All urbanizacions on the island were, before a single plot of land was sold, legally obliged to lay down piped water, metalled roads, street lighting, electricity, and telephones. One or two promoters were said actually to have honoured their obligations, but most were long on promises and short on performance. Since it was usually foreigners who bought such land no one – apart from the foreigners, of course – was in any way inconvenienced. However, the urbanizacion in which Casa Elba stood had been developed by a promoter with a social conscience and there were not only metalled roads which hadn't yet started to break up too badly, street lights, electricity points, no real reason why telephones should not be connected, and piped water which flowed except in bad droughts, there was also a man who was employed to tend the unsold plots, the verges, the rock garden, and the tennis courts.

Hevia was a tall, thin, balding man with a long, sad-looking face. He pushed to the back of his head the beret he wore in winter or summer and scratched his head with earth-stained fingers. 'It's like this, Inspector, most of the time I'm so busy I don't notice no one.'

Alvarez stared at the rock garden, set to the side of the steps, which was crowded with weeds. 'I can imagine. But maybe when you weren't quite so busy you noticed someone going into Casa Elba?'

'Casa Elba?' Hevia hawked and spat. 'That's the place where that miserable old beanstick of a woman lives.'

'That's right. She died suddenly.'

'So I heard tell.'

Two black vultures were riding the thermals high above the mountains. They really ought to settle over Casa Elba, thought Alvarez. 'It's beginning to look as if she was poisoned.'

Hevia showed no astonishment.

'So I want to know who was visiting her on Wednesday and Thursday. I thought you might have seen someone?'

Hevia dug his mattock into the lowest pocket of soil and then leaned on the handle. 'Wednesday or Thursday?' He stared at the ground.

Alvarez waited with endless patience. Because he was from the same background as Hevia, he could appreciate the other's need to consider the subject exhaustively before giving an answer: when one worked with the soil, one learned to rush nothing.

'I've seen someone,' said Hevia finally. He looked up.

'On which day?'

'It were the Wednesday.'

'D'you know who it was?'

'I reckon.'

'Who?'

'You.'

A superior chief from Madrid would have sworn loudly at such sly, stupid insolence, but Alvarez merely laughed. Hevia looked disappointed.

'Anyone else?' asked Alvarez.

'There were someone there on the Thursday.'

'Yeah. Me.'

'Didn't see you,' said Hevia, and he laughed.

'So who did you see?'

'There were a man on a bicycle who went down the slip road.'

'Did he go to her house?'

'There ain't no other house down that slip road, is there?'

'What I'm asking is if you saw him go into her house?'

'I just saw him bike down. I ain't got all day to do nothing but just stand around and watch.'

'About what time was this?'

'Just as it were getting dark.'

'Have you ever seen him around before?'

'No.'

'Can you describe him?'

There was another long pause. 'He was young, I reckon. Can't say more'n that.'

'What kind of hair?'

'Couldn've been any kind. It were getting dark and I was a ways away.'

'What was he wearing?'

'Clothes.'

Even Alvarez's patience was tried by that. 'What kind of clothes?' he demanded sharply.

When Hevia spoke, his voice showed his satisfaction at having annoyed the other. 'I wouldn't know. Like I told you . . .'

'It was getting dark,' interrupted Alvarez.

As Alvarez approached Ca'n Ritat he thought how little he liked the place. Set against the mountain backdrop, the house looked attractive, the garden was lovely and even at a poor time of the year was filled with colour, but the old farmhouse had been so drastically altered and re-built that little of the original was left and the flower garden was wasting good, rich soil which could have grown vegetables.

Orozco was in the kitchen garden directing water through irrigation channels drawn out of the soil with a mattock. Alvarez stood and watched the water lap round the onion plants as the channel was closed, then quickly drain away. 'I met an Englishman who reckoned that if we'd use good, modern seed on this island, we'd double our crops.'

'There's silly buggers everywhere.'

'I don't know so much. There've been tremendous strides in other countries in breeding hybrids which give better yields or are more resistant to disease. And we do tend to use the same strain of seed year after year. The experts'll tell you it's wrong to use seed from the same strain in the same ground twice or more.'

Orozco closed the last side channel. He trudged back to the main channel and altered the flow, with two mattockfuls of earth, so that now the water ran to beans. He straightened up and flexed his powerful shoulders.

'D'you ever meet an expert who got his hands dirty, doing the work? The señor gave me seed to plant. It won't do no good, I told him. Plant it, he orders, this is proper, expert seed from England. So I let him see me plant it and then when he'd gone I slung it. I wasn't going to waste my time. Our seed's used to sun and his seed's used to rain. Stands to reason his wouldn't have been no good out here.'

Alvarez had never before heard him speak so freely, but talk to any true peasant about land or animals and he becomes loquacious. 'But some of the newly developed seeds will stand up to a lot of sun even if they come from a climate like England's . . .'

'And when it grows up it comes with curl or rots or gets eaten by bugs,' said Orozco with contemptuous certainty.

There was both weakness and strength in a peasant's stubbornness, thought Alvarez, happy to associate himself with such stubbornness. It clung to tradition and refused to accept novelty: in a world which seemed to believe all tradition was nonsense and all novelty desirable, that was a valuable trait. 'How's the señora?' He jerked his thumb in the direction of the house.

'All right.' Orozco once more became taciturn. He went over to the beans and changed the flow of water to another long channel.

Alvarez, who'd followed, said: 'Is she over the shock of the señor's death?'

'Could be.'

'Has she heard how her brother-in-law is?'

'Couldn't say.'

'Is her husband back yet?'

'No.'

He sounded uninterested, yet this would not be so, Alvarez knew. It was just that in such matters he would be a complete fatalist because life had taught him that to worry changed nothing. Alvarez's mind changed tracks and he began to fidget with the button of his coat. 'Luis is a lot older than she is, isn't he? D'you reckon it matters very much?'

'I reckon it ain't none of my business.'

'They say that when a husband's a lot older than his wife, she gets restless. That sort of thing could cause trouble.'

Orozco said nothing.

'But I'd have thought an older husband meant he was steadier and didn't spend his time looking at other skirts. That could count for a lot.' Caroline would never become restless because she would give total loyalty . . . Had God robbed him of his few wits? Since when had rich, beautiful women ever looked at penniless peasants with anything but pity or scorn? He sighed. It seemed a man had no shield against his own foolish dreams. 'There's something I want to know. Did you see a stranger come to this place a day or two before the señor died? Someone you've never clapped eyes on before, or maybe only once. A chunky kind of a bloke with curly brown hair, in his early twenties, shoulders as solid as yours? Could've been dressed in kind of seaman's clothes.'

'Ain't see no one like that.'

'It's probable he was not in a car, but was riding a bicycle.'

'Ain't I just said no? If words were pesetas, you'd be bloody rich.'

'I've got to keep on asking. I've a job to do.'

'Then why not clear off and do it?'

Alvarez laughed.

The Mallorquin woman who lived in the flat next to Caroline said that she had gone to stay with an English friend. She didn't know who that friend was. Alvarez drove to the nearby supermarket where many of the English shopped and he asked the staff if any of them could tell him with whom Señorita Durrel was staying. One of the assistants said she thought the señorita was with Señora Jarmine who lived in a house in the urbanizacion which lay half-way between the Port and Llueso.

He drove to the urbanizacion. Here, the houses, perched on the mountainside, were large and luxurious, almost all with swimming pools despite the difficulty and great expense of building them because of the slope of the rock.

He disliked Señora Jarmine on sight. She was coarse and vulgar and she possessed to a fine degree that insulting, off-hand superiority which seemed to come so naturally to many English. He spoke with great politeness. 'May I speak with Señora Durrel, please? My name is Inspector Alvarez of the Cuerpo General de Policia.'

'Why d'you want to worry her now?' demanded Bertha.

They still stood in the hall. Anyone with any manners at all, he thought, would at least have taken him into the sitting-room. 'Señora, I must ask her certain things.'

'She's not up to being pestered by the police.'

'Señora, I am sure she will be able to answer for me the few questions I need to ask.'

'You'd better come back some other time.' She moved towards the front door.

'I regret very much, Señora, but I must speak to her now if she is here, in your house.' His tone remained polite, but there was the snap of authority to his words.

She looked at him with obvious annoyance. 'Wait.' She left, passing through an open archway.

He studied the hall. There were two Persian carpets, three paintings which could well have been old masters, to judge from their elaborate frames and sombre subjects, four very ornate antique pistols, a beautifully inlaid table with a patina that could have come only from constant care, and a striking group of two men and a dog in silver. How many cuarteradas of rich land did they represent?

Bertha returned. 'Go on in,' she said bad-temperedly, indicating the open archway. He went through. The sitting-room was very large and from the picture windows there was a view of the plain and Llueso Bay and to the west of that a small corner of Playa Nueva Bay and Puerto Playa Nueva which stood on the isthmus which separated the two mountain-ringed bays.

Caroline sat on the richly upholstered settee. In sharp contrast to Bertha, she wore a simple cotton frock, no jewellery other than a small locket which had been her mother's, and no make-up. She looked tired and strained and her voice was tense. 'It isn't true, is it? She wasn't poisoned? It's just another beastly rumour?'

He vainly longed to be able to shelter her from the beastlinesses of the world. 'Señorita, I am very sorry, but I cannot say. Until the tests are finished, I do not know.'

'Then you think it is possible she was poisoned?'

He nodded.

She shivered.

'Señorita, I will be as brief as possible, but there are some questions which I have to ask.' He sat down in one of the armchairs. 'I need to know something of Señorita Cannon's financial affairs. Will you be able to help me? Perhaps she has spoken to you about them?'

'Mabel never talked to me about anything like that.'

'Then you do not know if she was very wealthy?'

'She obviously had enough money to live on, but she didn't lead an expensive life. I'm sure she wasn't what I'd call very wealthy.'

'Do you know if she had relations on the island or in England?'

'I don't think so, because she never spoke of anyone. And there was something sad about her which always made me think she must be completely on her own.'

'I suppose, then, you cannot tell me who is likely to be her heir?'

'I've no idea.'

'Señorita, there is one other matter on which I have to ask you. When I last met you, I was leaving the señorita's house and you had driven up to it. I told you the señorita was disturbed and so I think you did not visit her. Did you see her before she died?'

'No. You see I thought it was best not to go to her place for a little. Mabel was rather . . . Well, she could get very excited over some things and then she wouldn't be quite reasonable.'

'Who was your friend who was with you in that car on Wednesday?'

She tried to answer casually, but was far too inept at dissembling her feelings to prevent her voice tightening. 'Edward Anson. He's a wonderful boatbuilder and is going into partnership with Ramón Mena.'

'Then he will be very successful. Ramón is a great craftsman, señorita . . . Were you perhaps wishing to speak to Señorita Cannon about something of importance?'

'No. Not really. We were just going to see her.'

'Are you sure you had not something of importance to discuss?' It was like hitting a blind man, he thought angrily.

'We . . .' She fiddled with a corner of her sleeve. 'It was just that we had an idea to talk over with her.'

'Perhaps the idea was for your friend?'

After a while, she nodded.

'And Señor Anson went back to speak to Señorita Cannon about this matter on Thursday?'

'Of course he didn't,' she said urgently.

'You are certain he did not speak to her in her house?'

'Quite, quite certain.'

'Will you tell me what was this matter you wished to discuss?'

'Teddy has to buy his partnership in the boatyard and Mabel said she would lend him the money.'

'But now? Do you know what will occur now, señorita?'

She shook her head. 'It all seemed so wonderful until . . . Teddy's always wanted to work in his own yard and this was the chance of a lifetime.'

'But now he has again to find the money to pay Ramón Mena?'

She nodded.

He thought for a moment, then stood up. 'I have disturbed you for long enough. Thank you for your kind help.'

'He didn't go back to see Mabel. I promise you he didn't.'

'I understand, señorita.'

He left and crossed the hall to the front door. Bertha came into the hall from a side room as he opened the door and he said goodbye to her. She merely nodded her head in curt acknowledgement.

He drove down to the Port and along the western arm of the harbour to the boatyard. Ramón Mena was in his office. He was short, no more than one and a half metres high, and his face was the colour of ancient, uncared-for mahogany, so creased it was as if he had suffered an endless succession of skin grafts. His eyes were dark brown and sharp and always on the move.

'Enrique! It's a long time since I saw you.'

'I've been sweating my guts out, working.'

Mena laughed. 'That'll be the day.'

'How's the wife?'

'Getting into a terrible state because Eulalia is to be married very soon.'

'Your niece? But she's no age.'

'Ask my sister-in-law and she'll tell you she's more than ready for marriage. It's you who's forgotten all the years. You're getting old.'

'Great news!... Ramón, I want to hear about the Englishman, Edward Anson. What's he like at working?'

'Good. When he prepares a wooden deck, you could eat a meal off it. If he scrapes down the superstructure, you won't find a millimetre of old varnish in any corner. Pride. That's what he's got. Pride in what he's doing. Not like most of the youngsters today who only worry about how long to knocking-off time.'

'Someone was telling me you'd offered him a partnership?'

'That's right. One and a half million in cash. Him and me could do great business together with the foreigners.' Mena stared shrewdly at Alvarez. 'Why should this interest you? Is it because of the death of the English?'

'It's just that I'm vaguely interested in Anson,' said Alvarez.

Mena grinned. 'Sure. Just vaguely.'

'How are things going for him with the partnership?'

'How should I know for certain until he arrives with the money?'

'But you think he'll be able to find that much?'

'He keeps telling me so.'

'You must have given him some sort of deadline?'

'Naturally. I told him a few days ago I must expand next season and for that I need the money so unless he pays a million and a half within two weeks I'll have to find someone else as a partner.'

'How did he react to that?'

'As always, he said he would find the money. I told him, I can't go on and on with nothing but promises. Then on Friday he came and said he would definitely get the money but it would take a little longer. Wanted to know if I'd extend the fortnight I'd given him.'

'Did you agree?'

'I said if it was certain this time, I'd try and wait.' As any Mallorquin would, Mena became bothered that it might seem to someone else as if he were getting the worst of the bargain. 'Understand, Enrique, he is a clever man with the boats.'

A clever man who had been faced with a deadline, thought Alvarez.

CHAPTER XV

Ambition, thought Alvarez, was like Janus, double-faced. He walked past a shop which had outside it baskets of beach sandals and beach balls and racks of snorkeling gear. Some men were exalted by ambition, some were destroyed.

Anson lived in a house along one of the small side streets which led off the Llueso road just before the limits of the Puerto. Here, the houses were terraced, yet each was different in design so that each possessed its own identity. Most had small courtyards where flowers grew the year round and even orange trees, despite the salt-laden air, were cosseted into bearing fruit.

He entered No. 7 and called out. An old woman, dressed in widow's black, entered the hall and she told him the señor was in his room at the back of the house. She led Alvarez through the kitchen into a small, paved court-yard and waved an arthritically deformed hand at the small caseta which formed the far side of the courtyard.

The caseta had two small rooms and Anson was in the first one. When he saw Alvarez, his expression tightened.

'Good afternoon, señor. I apologize for troubling you, but I wish to ask you some things.' Alvarez approached the table and stared down at a nearly completed waterline blueprint of a ketch. 'Are you going to build that?'

'I wouldn't know. It would probably bloody sink, anyway,' said Anson roughly.

Apart from the chair in which Anson sat, and from which he had not bothered to rise, there was a rocking-chair in traditional Mallorquin style. Alvarez sat down on this. 'I suppose you have heard about the unfortunate death of Señorita Cannon?'

'Of course. The bush telegraph works best with deaths.'

'It may be that she was poisoned. Have you heard that also?'

'Yes.'

'So it is my job to learn who maybe poisoned her.'

'We've all got to earn a living somehow.'

'You and Señorita Durrel were travelling to see her on Wednesday, were you not?'

'That seems a fair bet since you met us outside her house.'

'Was she a friend of yours?'

'Caroline liked her.'

'But I am asking how you found her?'

Anson jerked his head with an angry gesture. 'She and I agreed to differ on anything we could find to talk about.'

'Then I wonder why you were going to see her?'

'Because Carrie had persuaded me to.'

'If she had to persuade you, was it to be more than a social visit?'

'What the hell business of yours is it?' Anson looked belligerently at Alvarez and then saw a look in the detective's eyes which disturbed him enough to answer the question. 'I'd been offered a partnership in Mena's boat-yard and Carrie said Mabel would lend me the money I needed.'

'And you were prepared to accept this money from someone you very much disliked?'

'I'd take it from the devil, if he offered it.'

Alvarez knew a grudging admiration for Anson's honesty. 'When I met you, I told you that the señorita was very disturbed. I think you did not see her that evening?'

'No.'

'So you went to see her on the next day?'

Anson said forcefully: 'I never went back there.'

'You did not go and see her on Thursday and ask for the money you needed?'

'That's what I've just told you.'

'Then I wonder who it was on a bicycle who arrived at the señorita's house just before it became dark?'

'All I know is, it wasn't me.'

'If you had gone, I wonder what she would have said?'

'She could've said anything.'

'You are certain you did not go to her house on Thursday?'

'Of course I bloody am.'

'If you did not speak with the señorita, how can you be so certain when you speak with Ramón that you will have the money?'

'I wasn't. But I wasn't going to tell him that so that he offered the partnership to someone else.'

'On Friday you said it was certain. The señorita died on Friday so how could it then be certain?'

'I've just explained. Anyway, I didn't know she was dead.'

'You must have heard she was very ill?'

'Ill, yes, dying, no. If I'd known she was dead I wouldn't have been able to go on hoping I could buy that partnership, would I?'

'That depends, perhaps, on how well you can read Spanish.'

'What's that supposed to mean?'

'Do you read Spanish reasonably well?'

Anson hesitated. 'I can read it a bit.'

'Then if you had gone on your own to the señorita's house on Thursday, you might have read something which would have convinced you you could be able to pay the million and a half.'

'You're talking double Dutch.'

Alvarez rocked the chair forward and stood up. 'Señor, you will please make certain you do not leave the Port until I speak to say you may.'

'You've no right . . .'

'I have the right to do many things.'

'Why are you leaning on me like this?'

'I am investigating the deaths of Señorita Cannon and Señor Freeman. I think you can help me.'

Alvarez left. He walked through the main house, said goodbye to the old woman who was in the hall polishing a chair, and went out to his car. As he sat behind the wheel, he thought that ambition had smiled on Anson with both faces: first it had exalted, then it had destroyed.

CHAPTER XVI

Pablo Camponet had a round, cheerful face and a smile a mile wide. He spoke and wrote Castilian, Catalan, English, French, and German fluently and could converse reasonably in Swedish and Dutch. He had read Shakespeare, Goethe, and Hugo, in the original and he played the 'cello well enough for a visiting conductor of some note to try to get him to give up his job and take up music full time. His job was head waiter. He was always amused when foreigners, confident they could not be understood, referred to the ignorant locals.

After handing him the sheet of paper to read, Alvarez called a waiter over and ordered two brandies. When the waiter returned he put the glasses on the table and then, as he handed over the bill, winked. Alvarez was pleasantly surprised to discover that he had been charged a reasonable amount instead of the exorbitant sum he would have been had he been a tourist.

Camponet looked up. 'How much of this have you managed to understand?'

'Next to nothing, although I did make out it was to do with money.'

'It's a tontine.'

'What's that?'

'The idea was devised by a bloke in France some time back in the 1650's. Roughly speaking, several people paid the same amount of money into a fund which was put out at interest. The survivor drew the lot.'

Alvarez, who had been about to drink, whistled. 'Translate for me word by word, will you, Pablo?'

He listened carefully. The sum of 2,173,542 Swiss francs

had been deposited with the Banque de Foch. Each of the three partners would be nominally credited with a third of the capital and each could draw up to one-quarter of the total annual interest, but no further sum could be drawn without authority being given by all three in writing. Should any one partner die, his share of capital would be nominally divided between the remaining two, who could then each draw up to one-third of the annual interest. If there were only two partners, capital could be withdrawn on the signatures of both of them. On the death of the second partner, the capital and accumulated interest became the survivor's absolutely.

Camponet put the paper down on the table. 'I remember that there was one famous tontine in the eighteenth century, organized by an Italian adventurer called Viglianesi. He somehow persuaded eight sober, God-fearing, intelligent, rich men of Ferrara each to invest the modern-day equivalent of twelve million pesetas in an all-or-nothing tontine in which he was given a ninth share. Six of the eight died before anyone became curious and then it was only by mistake, so that really no one should ever have been alerted. They put Viglianesi to the question and in the end he admitted he'd been feeding his victims various poisons, including arsenic. The interesting thing about this tontine was that Viglianesi was known by the eight to be an adventurer, always on the look-out for a fast peseta, and yet they allowed him to persuade them to invest in the tontine and, when they started to die off, didn't report their suspicions. Why? Obviously because each was hoping to be the last survivor of the eight whereupon he could denounce Viglianesi and scoop the pool. It makes an interesting commentary on the ethics of the rich. I've often wondered which of the two finally survived to inherit – history doesn't relate. No doubt, he burned a candle or two for Viglianesi's soul.'

'You are a cynic.'

'What waiter isn't? You can't watch men, women, and especially children, shovelling food and drink down themselves for day after day and still believe good of your fellow humans . . . Has anything happened to anyone in this tontine?'

'I think that two of the members are now dead.'

'Leaving the third the happy and enriched survivor. You are surely talking about the two English who have recently died, from poisoning so rumour has it? History repeats itself. I trust you will put the survivor to the question.'

'First catch your tiger,' muttered Alvarez, remembering the recipe for tiger soup. How to identify the third person when so far it had proved impossible to discover the true identity of either Freeman or Mabel Cannon? Would the Banque de Foch now break its code of silence and so help the murder investigation? Was Anson number three? If he wasn't, then surely he must be innocent? Even if he had cycled to Casa Elba just as it was getting dark on Thursday . . .?

'Enrique, you look like a man with problems.'

'God's truth, I feel like a cement-mixer is churning round in my head.'

'Then you need another coñac.'

'I'd better not drink any more.'

'That's an admission of defeat.' Camponet called out to the barman for two more brandies.

Tonight, Alvarez thought, he had to report to Superior Chief Salas. What did he report? That half an hour ago he had known everything, but that now he knew nothing?

'Throw up your job which causes you such headaches and come and be a waiter at the hotel. I'll give you the best tables close to the serving hatches and I'll make certain all the good tippers sit with you. I'll not even take my usual percentage from your tips. You'll get rich and yet never have to think again.'

'Very humorous,' muttered Alvarez.

'Come on, man, where's your sense of humour?'

'I strangled it half an hour ago.'

Dolores, who stood in the centre of the room, put her hands on her hips. She glared at Alvarez. 'So! You tell me you just are not hungry.'

'You're blocking the television,' complained Ramez.

She ignored her husband. 'Perhaps my food is no longer good enough for you, Enrique?'

'It's not that . . .' began Alvarez, belatedly realizing that he had upset his cousin.

She interrupted him loudly. 'I spend the whole day slaving to prepare the dinner – when I could be sitting around like a grand lady, discussing the fashions in Madrid. Yet when I come to serve the meal, what happens? Tell me, what happens?'

'He said he wasn't very hungry, that's all,' pointed out Ramez.

She ignored him a second time. 'You do not want my food. Why not? Is it because I am only an ordinary cook who knows only ordinary Mallorquin food, good enough for your parents, but not for you since you have started mixing with foreigners?'

'It's nothing like that . . .'

'Fool that I was to waste so much of my time preparing a sopa Mallorquinas!'

'Not one of your very special, so delicious soups?' asked Alvarez, suddenly crafty.

'All my soups are special and delicious,' she retorted, with grand arrogance.

'Dead true. There's no one alive who can make a sopa Mallorquinas like you.'

'And tell me why I spent so much time at the butcher's choosing the pork chops when a piece of bad belly would have been sufficient?'

'You haven't prepared an ali-oli to go with the chops, have you?'

'Since when have I served pork chops without ali-oli? And tumbet?'

'Not tumbet as well?'

'Do you think I was prepared to have you starve? And then for hours I worked to make pastry as light as a puff of wind so that I could fill it with angel's hair jam because I was fool enough to want to give you a meal you would enjoy.'

'Have you made two for me?'

'Name the day when I have made only one! . . . But all is wasted. We will give the food to someone who is hungry.' She ran the palm of her hand over her jet black hair in a gesture of offended pride and then stamped out of the sitting-room to go to the kitchen.

Alvarez stood up and crossed to the low sideboard, where he poured out brandies for Ramez and himself.

'She's spitting tacks because the next-door neighbour's just bought a flashy vacuum cleaner and I've refused to get her one. I tried to tell her they're a waste of money and brush and dustpan's good enough for anyone, but you know women!' Ramez shrugged his shoulders. 'I must say, though, you look worn out. Are things tough at work?'

Alvarez returned to his chair. 'If they get any tougher, they'll be carrying me out feet first. I tell you, I even missed out on a siesta today.'

Ramez stared at him in amazement.

'It's the English. They're always the same. Foul up anything. If a Mallorquin gets killed, it's straightforward; if an Englishman gets killed, he makes certain he goes out like a corkscrew.'

'You sound really worried.'

'Look, Jaime, I'd got the whole thing worked out and then the English señorita gets herself killed and I had to start all over again. So I beat my brains out and discover who killed her. And what happens next?'

'Another corkscrew?'

'Another bloody corkscrew. And now I've got to find someone whose name I don't know, whose description I haven't got, who may live anywhere this side of hell, and who killed the other two for well over twenty-five million pesetas.'

Ramez whistled. 'Twenty-five million! Who wouldn't knock off a couple of people for that much?'

'I'll tell you one thing. If I had the chance I'd bump off all the English for nothing.'

Dolores came into the sitting-room and stared at Alvarez. 'You've room for litres of coñac, then, even if you've no room for my cooking?'

He stood up, crossed the floor, and kissed her on the cheek. 'When you started talking about the food you've been cooking, my appetite came back like a bomb. Right now, I'm starving.'

As they stood on the harbour arm, the light breeze just ruffling their hair, Caroline looked at Anson. He had the face of a man who would always be over-ready to fight, she thought. He'd square up long before there was any need. 'I'm sure you're wrong, Teddy.'

'Like hell I am.' He studied the yacht moored opposite to them. She was a racing job, with tear-drop hull, tall mast, a cockpit filled with large dial instruments, and coffee-grinder winches. She'd beat up to wind, with the sea boiling over her lee, like a bird in flight. At sea life might be hard, but it was always straightforward.

The sun was low and about to dip behind the mountains on the far side of the bay and in the slanted sunshine the set of his mouth looked even more stubborn. Would he go so far as to fight with murder . . . She shivered, hating herself for ever having posed the question.

'He all but accused me of murdering Mabel,' said Anson.

'I wonder if he really meant it as you've taken it? He seemed so nice when I've spoken to him.'

'Sure. And a boa-constrictor looks all cuddly until it comes up and cuddles you a little too tightly.'

'Teddy, why didn't you tell him you'd been to see Mabel? Why did you want me to lie about it?'

'If he knew for sure I'd been to her place on Thursday, I'd be for the high jump, wouldn't I?'

'Of course you wouldn't, since you didn't do anything.' She managed, for once, to keep her doubts out of her voice. 'And surely it's worse now when he seems to be so suspicious for some reason?'

'I don't care how suspicious he gets so long as he can't prove anything. Carrie, I've told you time after time, the world doesn't always smell of violets. Most times, it smells like a midden. If you'd told him you'd been to see Mabel, he'd have thought nothing of it. But if I'd admitted I had been, he'd have slammed the handcuffs on.'

'I'm sure he's not like that. He's the kind of man who would never do anything nasty unless he absolutely had to because he doesn't want to hurt anyone.'

'He was gunning for me in no small way. If I'd given him half a chance more, I'd have had my chips.'

'Why should he be gunning for you?'

'How in the hell should I know? I just know he is.'

Alvarez turned over in bed and told himself to relax so that he could get to sleep. But the same old questions came flooding back into his mind. Who were Freeman and Mabel Cannon? Assuming they had been in the tontine, where had the money come from, who was the third member? Anson? But if he were, he'd either not need a partnership in the boatyard or else he'd buy it without any trouble. Would the Swiss bank identify whoever it was? If the third person weren't identified very quickly, he was going to vanish along with a fortune . . . God damn the English, he thought, and finally fell asleep.

CHAPTER XVII

Anson was re-caulking the deck of a converted Grimsby trawler when he heard someone walk up the flimsy gangway which vibrated and set up a knocking noise. He looked round and saw Alvarez. His expression became bitter.

Alvarez, who hated the sea and could almost feel seasick on a boat tied up, walked round the high, thin wheelhouse. 'Good morning, señor. I went to your house to see you, but the señora told me you were working, even though it is a Sunday.'

Anson put down the caulking hammer. 'If I don't work when work's going, I starve. What about you?'

'I don't exactly starve, but I do have to explain to my senior who is a man not very inclined to listen.'

'And you're working now?'

'Yes, señor.'

Anson heaped up the loose oakum and stuffed it into a sack. 'Working at what? Putting the finger on me?'

'I wish merely to ask a few questions, to look at your passport, and then to drive you to meet two persons.'

'Who?'

'You will learn that later on.'

They got you by the short and curlies, thought Anson with bitter anger. In England, as often as not, you could tell them to take a running jump: in Spain, you did exactly as they said or you got the book thrown at you.

'Is there a room on this boat where we can sit and talk?'

'I suppose you mean a cabin?' As he spoke, Anson knew he was being stupid to go out of his way to antagonize the detective.

'I am afraid, señor, I often speak English badly.'

One of the Parelona ferries moved out of her night berth to sail round to the far side of the western arm where she would take on passengers. The deck hand who was aft shouted a greeting at Anson and he waved a brief acknowledgement.

'Shall we go downstairs?' suggested Alvarez.

'You mean below,' corrected Anson, before it occurred to him that this time the mistake had been deliberate.

A companionway led below to the saloon, which was large, with four ports on either side, bench seats, two moveable chairs which could be lashed down to the deck, a central table, and built-in cupboards.

Alvarez sat down, brought out a pack of cigarettes, and offered it. Anson hesitated, then finally took one. 'Sit down, señor.' He struck a match for both of them. 'Am I correct that you did not visit Señorita Cannon on Thursday?'

'I didn't go near her place,' answered Anson harshly.

'Do you know anything about her financial affairs?'

'I know nothing at all about her.'

'Would you think she was very rich?'

'If she was, she didn't spend it on herself. But she

obviously wasn't poor or she couldn't have made that offer to me.'

'Shall I surprise you if I say she was very rich, with a lot of money in the bank?'

'You'll surprise me.'

'Do you know who is her heir?'

'Probably some cats' home in Brighton.'

'Her will, written in Spanish, was in the desk in the sitting-room of her house. Did you not read it there?'

'I'm no bloody snooper.'

'Do you say you do not know who she has left her money to?'

'That's exactly what I've been saying for the past five minutes.'

'Where is your passport and residencia?'

'My passport's at the house.'

'And your residencia?'

Anson hesitated, then muttered: 'I haven't got one.'

'But I believe you have been in Spain since more than nine months?'

'What if I have?'

'Then you should have a residencia, señor. If you have no residencia, you can have no work permit. But to do work on this boat which is not yours, you need one.'

'All right. But I'm not the only person round this Port who's missed out on getting one.'

'Perhaps that is true, but you are the only person who I know for sure is working without a permit.' Alvarez was gratified to see the look of perplexed annoyance on Anson's face. 'When did you leave England?'

'A few years ago: something like five.'

'Where did you live and what name did you use when you were last in England?'

'What are you getting at now?'

'Just answer my questions.'

'I lived in Rexton Cross and surprise, surprise, I called myself Edward Anson. But I suppose I'd better confess to a criminal record. When I was at school I scrumped apples and one day I broke three windows in the school with my catapult and, real sneaky, never owned up.'

'Such a criminal record, señor, will be looked at kindly.'

Anson stood up and crossed the saloon to the galley which lay immediately aft and from there he brought an old tin in which he stubbed out his cigarette. He supposed he was being mocked, yet the detective's manner remained so solemn and correct that he couldn't be certain.

'If someone were to ask in the village of Rexton Cross about the young señor who stole apples and broke windows, what do you think he would be told?'

'Probably that when I left after my mother died it was good riddance to bloody bad rubbish.'

'But people would remember you?'

'They'd likely do that all right.'

Anson, thought Alvarez, sounded as if he were speaking the truth, which meant he had an identifiable past in England, unlike Freeman or Mable Cannon. 'Señor, will you now please come with me in my car?'

'Where to?'

'To meet Señor Hevia who works in the Llueso urbanizacion looking after the land which is not yet built on and the gardens which are for everyone.'

'Where's the point in me meeting him?'

'He saw a man on a bicycle visit Señorita Cannon on Thursday and he will be able to identify him. When he meets you he will be able to say it was not you – since you tell me this – and so I do not have to worry again.'

'It was too dark for him to see clearly.'

'But surely you cannot know how dark or light it was since I have not told you the time?'

Anson cursed himself for so rudimentary a mistake. 'Shall we go, señor?'

Anson bunched his fists and sat very upright. Then he relaxed, stood up, picked up the tin in which he'd stubbed out the cigarette, and said: 'I'll have to clear the deck before I leave.'

Alvarez left the saloon first. He went ashore and along to his parked car and sat behind the wheel. Surely, Anson was a fighter, the kind of man who sought out trouble with his fists, not poison?

They stopped outside Anson's house and Anson went in to get his passport. Alvarez examined it. The number was not consecutive with those of Freeman and Mabel Cannon. He wrote this down, together with the details, then handed the passport back.

They drove up the main road to the new football ground and there turned right to carry on to Ca'n Ritat. Alvarez parked level with the courtyard and as he climbed out of the car the dog came forward to the limit of its chain, barking and wagging its tail.

'Why've we come to this place?' asked Anson. 'You said we were going to the urbanizacion.'

'I wish to speak to the señora who used to cook for Señor Freeman.'

'This is Freeman's place?'

'You did not know that?'

'D'you think he invited the likes of me?'

'You might have arrived uninvited.' Alvarez climbed out of the car. He waited until Anson was out, then said: 'Wait here, I will not be long.' He crossed to the courtyard, patted the dog a couple of times on its head, then carried on to the kitchen. The door was opened by Matilde who was smiling and gay, the reason for her gaiety becoming obvious when she introduced him to her husband who had arrived in Palma that morning on the ferry from Barcelona.

Blanco was not wearing black, nor was she, so Alvarez asked: 'Your brother is better?'

'Thanks to God and a miracle, señor, he is now out of danger. The doctor says he will get better and better and by the time of The Three Kings he will be quite fit once again.'

'That's wonderful news! Tell me, how was Barcelona?'

'How is any city? Too many people, too much traffic, too little air to breathe.'

'You old stick-in-the-mud,' Matilde said, making the word 'old' one of endearment. 'Didn't you enjoy all the shops and the cinemas?'

He dismissed them with a quick shrug of his shoulders. He looked at Alvarez with a sudden uneasiness, drew in a deep breath, and said: 'Matilde tells me the señor died from eating a llargsomi?'

'That's right.'

'You must understand, señor, it was not among the esclatasangs. Lopez could not pick a llargsomi and Matilde could not cook one if he did. No one born on this island could ever pick or cook a llargsomi instead of an esclatasang if he thinks what he is doing.'

They stared at him, Blanco with timid challenge, Matilde worrying that he would take umbrage at her husband's attitude. After a short while he said: 'The llargsomi had to come from somewhere. So perhaps someone entered the kitchen during the evening – when the dog was barking so – and put the llargsomi among the esclatasangs when your wife was out.'

'Why should someone wish to kill the señor?'

'For his money, perhaps.'

'He was certainly a rich man.'

'Look, will you both do something for me that'll help? Go over and look through that window at the bloke who's by my car. Tell me if you've ever seen him around here before.'

Matilde looked at her husband as she instinctively waited for him to take the lead. After a moment he walked over to the window and she joined him there and together they stared out at Anson.

Alvarez waited, not surprised when they took a long time to decide. 'No,' said Blanco finally. 'We've not clapped eyes on him here.'

'That's right,' she confirmed. 'I've never seen him before.'

Alvarez sighed. 'I'm beginning to think it's not only the good Lord who works in riddles . . . Is Orozco here today as it's a Sunday?'

'No, señor. He never comes on a Sunday.'

'Can you tell me where he lives, then, so I can go and have a word with him?'

'In Calle Binissalem, but I don't know what number,' replied Blanco.

'That's all right, I'll soon find out. Thanks a lot for all your help.'

'Señor,' said Blanco, his voice urgent, 'there can't have been a llargsomi among the esclatasangs when Matilde took them from Lopez. You have to understand there just can't have been.'

Alvarez nodded. 'I understand that. But I also understand that there was one among them when Señor Freeman cooked his supper.'

She reached out and gripped her husband's hand. 'But . . . but who would do such a thing? It is such a terrible way to die.'

They stared at him, bewildered and afraid.

When he returned to the car, Anson said: 'I was beginning to think you were stopping here for lunch.'

'Unfortunately, señor, it often takes time to check up

on things.' Alvarez climbed in behind the wheel, started
the engine, and drove off as soon as Anson had secured
the seat-belt around himself. It would have been so much
simpler, Alvarez thought regretfully, if either Blanco or his
wife had said yes, they'd seen the Englishman at the house
and there'd been a devil of a row between him and the
señor.

Calle Binissalem was a short, rising street which
joined two of the main east to west roads which ran into
Llueso from the east. The houses were small and pressed
tightly together, yet all the doors, windows, and shutters,
were either newly painted or oiled and although it was
clearly a street where the poorer people lived, there was
no hint of poverty along its length.

Two boys who were playing football in the road told
Alvarez where Orozco lived and he parked just beyond
the front door. He told Anson to wait, promising that this
time it would be only for a moment, and left the car. He
stepped into the entrance hall, which was also the living-
room, and called out.

Orozco came out of the back room. He was wearing a
tattered pair of trousers and a torn shirt which was unbuttoned to show a thick vest underneath. He had not
shaved and his stubble was dark. 'What d'you want?' he
demanded surlily.

'A bit of help.'

He stared at Alvarez. 'Who told you where I live?'

'Luis Blanco.'

'Then he's back?'

'He came over on the night ferry. He says his brother
is on the mend and should be fit by The Three Kings.'

Orozco walked over to the table on which stood an
aspidistra in a brass pot and he picked up a pack of
cigarettes which he offered. 'You smoke?' When Alvarez
had taken a cigarette, he said: 'D'you want a coñac?'

'I'd not say no.'

'You've the look of a man who wouldn't know how.' He returned to the far room and when he reappeared he had two large glasses, three parts filled with brandy.

Alvarez drank. 'There's nothing like a coñac to put fresh life into a bloke.'

'You reckon you need some fresh life?'

'I need something and that's fact.' He nodded towards the window. 'I mustn't be long. I've an Englishman in the car and he'll be getting impatient if I don't go out soon.'

'They're born impatient.'

'Was that how Señor Freeman was?'

'Him? Plant a seed today and he'd want to harvest it tomorrow.'

'Maybe he was used to English seeds.'

Orozco suddenly grinned.

Alvarez drained his glass. 'Come outside and have a look at the bloke in my car and tell me if you've ever seen him hanging around Ca'n Ritat.'

They went out. The two boys who were playing football shouted that the enemy was in sight and they must scatter. Orozco waved his arms at them and one of them grabbed the ball and ran back a few yards, followed by the other, both laughing. 'Are you always the enemy?' asked Alvarez curiously.

'I fought for the other side, didn't I? Their parents have taught 'em to shoot me at sight.'

He spoke as if it were a matter of no consequence, yet Alvarez wondered if at heart he mustn't be saddened by the fact that not even forty years had been long enough to wash away the odium of having fought for the losing side.

Orozco stood in the road – there was no pavement – and stared at Anson in the car. Anson stared back at him through the windscreen.

'Never clapped eyes on him before,' said Orozco.

'OK. Thanks for the drink and smoke.'

Orozco stared once more at Anson, then turned and went back into the house. The two boys cheered. Alvarez climbed into the car.

'So who in the hell was that?' demanded Anson.

'The gardener at Ca'n Ritat. I wondered if he'd ever seen you around. He hadn't.'

'So now you're satisfied?'

'Not yet.'

Alvarez turned left at the bottom of the street into the one-way road which led out to the bridge over the torrente and the Puerto road. They reached the urbanizacion and drove along the slip road to Casa Elba, outside where Hevia was waiting for them.

As they stopped, Alvarez said: 'Get out and stand in front of the car.'

'Why?'

'Señor Hevia saw the person on a bicycle who came to visit the señorita on Thursday. When he tells me that that person could not possibly have been you, then finally I can be certain you did not come here on Thursday.'

Anson tried to appear to be as carelessly confident as before, but he could not hide all the signs of sudden tension. He opened the passenger door and climbed out on to the drive and stared challengingly at Hevia, but jammed his hands into his pockets to keep them out of sight in case they began to shake.

Alvarez walked over to Hevia. 'You saw a man coming to this place on Thursday on a bicycle. Was this the bloke?'

Hevia stepped forward to study Anson at no more than a couple of metres distance. After a while, he said: 'That's him.'

'Before, you couldn't describe him clearly, yet now you're quite certain?'

'I ain't good at describing, but I'm good at recognizing.'

'If it is dark . . .' began Anson in Spanish, muddling up the tense.

'Be quiet,' snapped Alvarez.

'There ain't no doubt,' said Hevia. 'D'you reckon he's the bloke what . . .'

'Thanks for your help. You can get off home now.'

Annoyed by this curt dismissal, since he was a man who prided himself on knowing about everything that went on in the urbanizacion, Hevia walked over to his Mobylette. He sat on it, pedalled to start the engine, then pushed it off the stand and drove away.

'We will go into the house,' said Alvarez. He led the way along to the front door, unlocked this, and went inside. He opened the shutters and left the windows open since the day was warm and the house needed airing.

Anson, who stood in front of the fireplace, said loudly: 'He was wrong. I don't give a damn what he says, I never came near the place on Thursday . . .'

'Señor, one moment before you complicate everything still more.' Alvarez sat down in one of the battered armchairs. He rested his elbows on the arms and his chin on his clasped hands. 'Until now, I could not be certain. Perhaps it was you who was on the bicycle, perhaps it was not. But now I know it was you.'

'Because that old fool says it was? When it was almost dark. You yourself told him just now that he couldn't describe me. So just how good is this sudden memory? No bloody good at all. But you're gunning for me and you're jumping to take anybody's word if it puts me in the dirt.'

'Señor, all I am concerned with is the truth,' said Alvarez, with a shade too much emphasis. 'Señor Hevia is certain it was you on the bicycle once he sees you again. I became even more certain when I remember Señorita

Durrel has said you did not see Señorita Cannon again after Wednesday.'

'In the name of hell, if she says I didn't see her again, how can that begin to make you so sure?'

'Unfortunately, the señorita is not good at lying because she is too honest. So when she lies it is obvious and she was lying when she told me that. I now know for certain that you saw Señorita Cannon here on Thursday.'

Anson, his square chin thrust forward, opened his mouth to argue further, then accepted the futility of this and closed it. He stamped over to the french windows, turned his back on the room, and stared out. The minutes passed and finally he said, so loudly he was almost shouting: 'All right, it was me on that bike.'

'Then why have you denied this until now?'

'Isn't that too bloody obvious for words? I'm hard pressed to find two pesetas to rub together, I haven't got a residencia or a work permit, and most of the English out here reckon I'm the kind of bloke who lost 'em their empire. I'm a sitting patsy for trouble.'

'But you are in very great trouble when you are discovered to be lying.'

'I took a gamble.' He shrugged his shoulders. 'But I wasn't born lucky, so I lost.' He swung round. 'Get this straight, though. I didn't poison the old girl and you're not hanging her death on me even if you'd like fine to do so.'

Alvarez spoke with immense dignity. 'I am a policeman and with no wish other than to discover the truth.'

'That'll be the day. What's the matter? I'm poor, I don't wear decent clothes, my uncle wasn't a duke, and I didn't go to some pansy school, so I'm a slummy who ought to be slung off the island!'

'Señor, in Spain such things are of no account. It is only the person and how he behaves which is important and it is insulting to suggest otherwise.'

The threat was unspoken, yet clear. Anson mumbled an apology and then went over to the second armchair and slumped down in it. Now his anger was shot, he cursed himself for a fool for being so ill-advised as to antagonize the detective after having to admit he had lied.

'What happened when you came to this house?'

'I told Mabel I must have a word with her.' Anson was silent for a while as his memory took him back. His expression became bitter. 'As soon as I was inside I realized I'd made the mistake of the year in not taking Carrie's advice and staying away. Mabel was twice as bitchy as usual. Went for me all ends up before I'd hardly said a word. Told me I'd pulled the wool over Carrie's eyes, but hadn't pulled it over hers. D'you know something?' His voice expressed his own incredulity. 'Instead of telling her to drop dead, I tried to explain everything, to tell her the strength of my ambition, to promise that if I could have the chance to realize that ambition I'd work myself into the ground.'

'She couldn't understand a vision?' said Alvarez.

'Didn't want to.'

'And then?'

Anson fiddled with one of his sideburns. 'She really took off. Shouted she wouldn't lend a single peseta to a boat-bum who was only any good at living off other people.'

'How did you react to that?'

'I was never good at turning the other cheek. Trouble is, I haven't any party manners because I crawled out from under the bottom drawer . . . I told her a few home truths.'

'And she did what?'

'Slung a paperweight at me.'

Surprised, Alvarez suddenly remembered how she had thrown a table at him. 'Did she hit you?'

'Missed by feet, thank God, or she'd have brained me.'

'Where did this paperweight hit?'

'The wall over there. Like as not you can still see the mark.'

Alvarez stood up and crossed to the wall to examine it.

'More to the right.'

He found the point of impact, marked by an indentation in the plaster from which radiated a number of small cracks. 'It must have hit very hard. As you said, it was a good job that she missed you. After she had thrown this paperweight, did you leave?'

'What the hell do you think? It might have been something bigger the next time.'

'And, of course, you no longer had the chance of borrowing the money you so needed?'

'My middle name has always been tactless.'

'You seem to speak as if all this did not matter. But afterwards you must have been very sad it happened?'

'Being sad didn't alter anything, did it?'

'No, señor. But perhaps you were sad enough to think very hard and you decided that there was one thing which could still help you?'

'Such as what?'

'Señorita Cannon's death.'

'How could her death alter the fact that I wasn't going to get a single peseta out of her?'

'Not out of her, no, but perhaps out of Señorita Durrel since she was named heir in the will which was in that desk over there and which you read.'

'I'm no snooper. And d'you bloody think I'd drag Carrie into it . . .' Anson came to his feet, fists clenched.

Alvarez spoke calmly. 'Señor, remember that in this country it is a serious crime to hit a policeman.'

Anson slowly lowered his hands. 'Don't worry,' he sneered, 'I never hit old men.'

Alvarez very nearly stood up and hit him.

CHAPTER XVIII

The Telex message from England was received at eleven forty-seven on Monday morning.

Reference Freeman and Cannon. Latest enquiries suggest Freeman was born Geoffrey Castle and Cannon, Mabel Striggs. Castle and Striggs worked H. G. Hoffman & Sons, Castle as firm's accountant and Striggs in computer division. Misinformation fed into computer four years nine months ago resulted in bogus payments made of total £232,762. Striggs under suspicion when she, Castle, and Brent vanished. Castle deserted wife and two children. Enquiries failed to trace them, though believed on Continent. Charles Brent: aged 23, height 1 metre 75, dark brown hair worn long and curled, full beard and moustache, face oval, eyes light blue and regular, eyebrows arched and prominent, nose triangular, mouth small, lips full, dentures, chin weak with cleft, ears slightly bat-wing and pointed with long lobes, body thin, shoulders rounded, fingers long and thin, prints and photograph available. Please send photographs and prints Freeman and Cannon. Advise if any information Brent.

Alvarez phoned the local branch of the Caja de Ahorros y Monte de Piedad de Las Baleares and asked them to tell him the exchange rate between the pound and the Swiss franc four years nine months previously. There was a short wait before he was given the answer. He multiplied 232,000 by 6.5 and the answer was just over a million and a half. The pound had depreciated, Freeman and Mabel Cannon had bought houses ... Their passports, both forged, bore consecutive numbers, they had arrived together, nothing was known about their past and no friends from England were known to have visited them ... Fingerprints would confirm, but at this stage Alvarez had no doubt that their true identities were now known. He visualized the awkward, foolish Mabel Striggs, infatuated with Castle, gradually being seduced into the crime. And the younger Brent, probably cocksure, seduced not by love but by fortune ...

Anson did not fit the description of Brent. Either Brent had murdered Freeman and Mabel Cannon (it was easier to think of them by the names they had had locally) to gain the tontine or Anson had murdered Mabel Cannon because she had left all her money to Caroline ... How could Brent have visited Ca'n Ritat, as surely he must have done, and discovered not only the routine of the house but also that Freeman liked esclatasangs, without the Blancos learning about the visit? If Anson had murdered Mabel Cannon it must be presumed he had read the will naming Caroline sole heir once Freeman was dead, but wouldn't he also have read, with the aid of a dictionary if necessary, the document setting out the tontine, and wouldn't he then have realized that when Mabel was dead she was no longer rich because the third man took all ...?

Mother of God, he thought, the ordinary brain was not made for such complications. He poured himself out a brandy.

Obviously, the most likely course of events was that Brent had murdered both victims in pursuit of the tontine. So, somehow he had been clever enough to avoid being seen by either the Blancos or Orozco. Difficult, yet certainly not impossible.

If Brent were the murderer, Anson was innocent. And yet he, Enrique Alvarez, had pursued Anson with a vindictiveness which at the time he had told himself was motivated by the desire to see justice done, but which now could be seen as motivated solely by jealousy. The pathetic jealousy of a middle-aged, soon-to-be-pot-bellied, peasant.

One thing now had to be done (it could not salve his pride – nothing could – but it would bring an end to the sorry events). He must find Brent and unmask him as the murderer. If Brent had settled in Spain, it would be possible to track him down quickly by assuming that his entry date (given when he applied for a residencia) would have been roughly the same as that of Freeman and Mabel Cannon. The fingerprints of his two index fingers would be on record and these could be compared with the prints from England. If he had settled in some other part of Europe, it should still be possible though it might take longer. Only if he had settled outside Europe . . . But as Freeman and Mabel Cannon's passports had had con-secutive numbers, wasn't it likely that Brent's either followed or preceded theirs, since all three would have been procured at the same time?

Tuesday was a miserable day. There was no rain, yet the clouds stretched from horizon to horizon and were a dirty, unwashed colour, becoming black over the mountains. The bay, so brilliantly blue in sunshine, was a tired green. The mountains which ringed the bay were dark, dismal grey.

Alvarez stood on the curving western arm of the harbour and stared at the yachts and motor-boats. For him, they epitomized the luxury of life he would never experience – a cynic would have said that for this he should be thankful in view of his susceptibility to sea-sickness.

'That one is for sale,' said Mena, who unheard had walked up to where he stood. 'She will cost you only twelve million pesetas if you bargain a little and in her you can sail from end to end of the Mediterranean. Or if you long to feel the blast of ocean winds, to cross the Atlantic and the Pacific.'

Alvarez turned and faced Mena, who looked thoroughly uncomfortable in a dark suit. 'If I had twelve million, I'd buy many cuarteradas of land and grow oranges, lemons, figs, almonds, algarrobas, trefoil, barley, wheat, oats, beans, tomatoes, potatoes, cabbages, cauliflowers, peppers, aubergines . . .' He became silent.

'Dreams!' said Mena. 'They keep a man alive . . . Shall I tell you the one truth I have learned in sixty-one years?'

'No. I'm feeling dismal already.'

'If a man gains his dreams, his life becomes worth-less.'

'I'll just go off and cut my throat.'

'Wait a little . . . D'you know what the owner of that yacht does with his life?'

'If he's English, he chases either little boys or big girls.'

'He is English and he drinks himself to death. So his beautiful yacht lies there, week after week, bare-poled, halyards fraying, riding nothing bigger than the harbour waves. I can feel her slowly dying from boredom because a man realized all his dreams and his life became worth-less.'

'You've been boozing.'

'My niece gets married this afternoon and so she is weeping, my sister-in-law is weeping, and my wife is weeping. A man needs a sou'wester and oilskins to remain in the house. Come and have a drink with me now.'

'You'd better not get any more plastered or Lucia will give you absolute hell.'

'How true . . . I often give thanks to God that I did not marry my wife's sister which I once considered . . . Though I've never mentioned that fact to Maria . . . Come on, Enrique, let's drink to the poor man who is marrying into such a watery family.'

They went through the main gateway and into Mena's office. Mena brought out of a cupboard a bottle of Carlos I brandy. 'You're still doing yourself all right, then,' said Alvarez.

Mena filled two large tumblers. 'If a man owns a beautiful yacht which never sails the seas, he should be made to pay for being such a fool.'

Alvarez sipped the brandy and wished that he owned a boatyard which had stupid, rich foreigners as customers.

'I have something important to tell you, Enrique.' Mena leaned back in his chair. 'Soon, I shall have a partner and we will expand and build yachts for people who are not stupid.'

'Is the Englishman, Anson, definitely joining you, then?'

'He came to me this morning and said that now everything was certain and he will be lent the million and a half. It will take a little time, but it will be.' Mena suddenly looked sharply at Alvarez. 'Do you think it is that sure?'

'It's no good asking me. I don't know anything about anything these days.'

'I hope it is so. With him, we will build the most beautiful yachts in the world.'

'And sail away to the Atlantic and the Pacific?'

'Not me. Maria does not like to sail and I have become too old to go on my own.'

'You'll be rich, so find a couple of young blondes for company.'

'At our age, Enrique, a young blonde does one no good.'

'Here, speak for yourself, old man.'

'Now I know that it is not cabbages and cauliflowers that you truly dream about.'

Alvarez emptied his glass and passed it over. 'Give me another or I'll start weeping even more than Maria and Lucia.'

'I went and saw Ramón,' said Anson.

'What did he say?' asked Caroline excitedly.

He stood up and began to pace the length of Bertha Jarmine's sitting-room. 'Being a Mallorquin, he tried to start talking about interest if the money wasn't paid right away, but he's a decent old stick at heart and he was in a sentimental mood because his niece is getting married so in the end he said OK.'

'Then you're a partner! Oh, Teddy, isn't it wonderful! I told you from the beginning your name would be going up outside the yard, didn't I?'

He stopped and faced her. 'I still hate the thought of taking the money from you.'

'But we've been all over that. I'm not going to give it to you, it'll be a loan, drawn up by a solicitor because that's what you want. It's a straight business deal.'

Her enthusiasm and vulnerable beauty raised a lump in his throat. 'When I've paid you back, Carrie, and we're building yachts for oil sheiks . . .' He stopped as Bertha came into the room and his expression was momentarily angry.

'D'you want a drink, Teddy?' Bertha asked. She was dressed in a see-through blouse and very tight pink trousers: only she could have worn such clothes without appearing completely vulgar.

'No, thanks. I've got to get back to the Port.'

'Are you starting as a partner right away?' Caroline asked.

'In name only.' He smiled sardonically. 'Ramón made that absolutely clear. No share of profits until the last peseta is paid in – until then I work for as small a wage as he dares offer.'

'I've already asked the solicitor to be as quick as possible.'

'But it's bound to take time.'

'You can borrow . . .'

'I'm not borrowing another peseta.' He crossed the room to the door. 'Be seeing you, Carrie. So long, Bertha.' He left.

Bertha walked over to the cocktail cabinet. 'Your usual?' Caroline nodded and she poured out a sweet vermouth and a gin and tonic. 'Carrie, I'm going to say something because I've a big mouth and I've had four husbands, which makes me an authority on bastards. Teddy could be trouble.'

'That's ridiculous. Why does everyone go on and on slandering him? Why don't you like him?'

'Don't get me wrong, I've never said I dislike him. He's a great big hunk of he-man and I could get goose-pimply wondering just how much of a man he could be. But I'm old and seasoned and know how to look after myself. You don't. And I'd hate like hell for you to get hurt.' She envied Caroline because Caroline was young and still knew ideals, yet for once her envy raised only a desire to protect, not sharp jealousy.

'What on earth d'you think can happen to me?'

'He can hit you very hard financially.'

'No. I can trust him absolutely.'

Bertha brought over the drinks. She handed one glass to Caroline, then went to a chair and sat down. 'Money comes too hard to take any risks and it's a girl's lifeline, even if diamonds are her best friend. So if you do get anything much from Mabel's will, for God's sake hang on to every penny. After all, if the partnership in the boat-yard were such a good proposition, wouldn't the banks have lent him the money?'

'He's no security to offer.'

'And they reckon he's a bad risk without security?'

'I don't care what they reckon. I just know that he himself is security enough for ten times what I'm lending him.'

Bertha sighed. 'All right, so you've made up your mind. But have you also thought how hard he can hurt you emotionally? Carrie, true knights in shining armour are becoming mighty thin on the ground: most of 'em are false and their armour's made of tin.'

'They're around if you're prepared to see them.'

'How much do you really like him?'

'A lot,' answered Caroline proudly.

Bertha drank, knowing she was defeated.

On Thursday morning, the corporal stepped inside the Club Llueso and checked the bar. When he saw Alvarez, he laughed loudly. 'I offered two to one you'd be here.'

'So you've made a fortune?'

'Give over. D'you think anyone would bet against a cert? I think I'll just have a coffee and a coñac.'

He went over to the bar to order. He returned to the table after being handed the brandy and sat opposite Alvarez. 'There's a message for you come through from the Peninsula. It seems pretty urgent.'

'Any idea what its gist is?'

'You've asked for enquiries to be made about a bloke. They've turned him up under a different name.'

'Where abouts is he?'

'Cala San Pedro. No one I asked knew the place so I looked it up on the map. It's roughly half-way along

Rosas Bay and looks pretty small.'

'Do they give any details about the bloke?'

'Nothing except to say that the dabs are his and that the name he's using now is . . . Don't remember exactly, but it's something like Snow. I've put the full text on your desk.'

The bartender brought over the corporal's coffee. Alvarez poured the rest of his brandy into his coffee. If Brent didn't panic and fly – and why should he? – all that remained to be done now was to question him and close the case. And once it was closed, there would be no further occasion for meeting Caroline Durrel. What had Mena said? If a man gained his dreams, his life became worthless. Only an old and rather drunken cynic would ever talk such rubbish . . .

The corporal interrupted his thoughts. 'You need a hearing aid. I've been speaking to you for the past few minutes and all you've done is stare into space. What's up?'

'I'm worrying about my soul.'

'For God's sake, drink up and forget such trivia.'

Perhaps that was the only sensible advice he had heard in days.

Alvarez, at the desk in his office, read the message. Fingerprints showed Charles Brent was now known as Peter Shore and he lived at No. 5, Calle Resons, Cala San Pedro.

He telephoned Superior Chief Salas. 'Señor, I have just received information that Charles Brent, now known as Peter Shore, is living in Cala San Pedro. That's a small place . . .'

'I know perfectly well where it is.'

'Of course! Since he is the surviving member of the tontine, he needs to be closely questioned regarding his movements over the past few weeks. I would respectfully suggest that a request, which had better be in your name, be sent to the Guardia at Cala San Pedro . . .'

'It will be much more satisfactory – I hope – if you fly over and interrogate him yourself.'

'Me, Señor? But I . . .'

'By the next plane.' The line went dead.

Alvarez slowly replaced the receiver. He hadn't left the island in years. He had never flown in his life . . .

'Santa Antonia,' he murmured, 'am I then so great a sinner?'

Alvarez carefully watched the engine on the starboard wing, but after ten minutes it still had not burst into flames. He relaxed a little and might even have learned to suffer, if not enjoy, flying had he not in his newfound confidence asked the air stewardess for a brandy and been asked to pay fifty pesetas for a drink which hardly covered the bottom of the glass.

They landed in driving rain. A bus took them to the terminal building and, since he had no luggage other than one overnight case, he did not have to wait for the baggage to come through. Outside the arrival area a Guardia was waiting for him.

'Inspector Alvarez? What a day you've chosen! It's been like this since dawn. I suppose Mallorca's in sunshine?'

It had been cloudy and threatening rain, but Alvarez answered loyally, 'It was warm enough to have to carry my coat as well as my mackintosh.'

'You blokes don't know how lucky you are! . . . The commissaire said you'd want me to drive you to Cala San Pedro first of all?'

'That's right. I want to question the Englishman, Shore.'

'He's not the bloke in Calle Resons?'

'That's right. You know him, then?'

'You're a bit late, Inspector. He's been dead over six months.'

CHAPTER XIX

Alvarez sat as close to the electric fire as he could get and gloomily listened to the commissaire.

'If the original enquiry had been sent to us, Inspector – as one might have expected – we would have given you all the details. Instead, I gather it was put through the register of foreigners so inevitably their records were hopelessly out of date.'

'They ought to have known, though. You say Brent – Shore – died back in March.'

The commissaire looked at Alvarez with impatient condescension. These provincial islanders clearly had no idea how official government departments worked. 'What did you want to question him about?'

'To tell the truth, I thought he was responsible for a couple of murders – but as these happened during the past three weeks, I obviously couldn't be more wrong.' He held out his hands to the fire which seemed to be giving less and less heat. 'How did he die, Señor?'

The commissaire opened a folder with a quick flick of his fingers: he was a man of precise, flicking movements. 'He owned a house in the urbanizacion to the east of the village. His maid went there in the morning as usual and found him crumpled up at the foot of the stairs, dead. There was an opened bottle of brandy in the sitting-room, together with a half-filled glass. The bathroom was up-stairs so it was clear that he had been up to that and was returning downstairs when, because he had drunk so much, he tripped and fell, to land on his head.'

'Was there a PM?'

'Naturally. He died from severe head wounds. His blood alcohol level was point four so he was very close to passing out before he fell.'

'That seems as if it was straightforward enough.'

'It was straightforward,' amended the commissaire.

'What's happened about his estate?'

'He had made a Spanish will and in this he left everything he owned to a woman called . . .' He looked down at the folder. 'Hilda Guelden. Her address was given as the same as his, but at the time of his death no woman was living with him. Neighbours remember an attractive blonde whom they thought was Dutch, but no one had seen her for at least a month before his death and one of these witnesses mentioned a row between the woman and Shore. Enquiries are still going on trying to trace Hilda Guelden.'

'Have you any idea how much the estate amounts to?'

'There was roughly fifty thousand in his bank, the house, and a car.'

'That's all?'

'It is.'

'How did he get his income?'

'He frequently paid into his bank fairly large sums.'

'Where did they come from?'

'We don't know, nor have we regarded this point as being of any importance.'

The commissaire was right, thought Alvarez, but not for the reason he believed. It was not a matter of importance because the source was known – the tontine. And when Charles Brent had died, his share of the tontine had been halved between Freeman and Mabel Cannon. And when Freeman had died everything had become hers.

And when she had died . . .

The commissaire flicked the folder shut. 'Of course, if you'd bothered to contact us in the first place, your journey today wouldn't have been necessary.'

'Ah well, señor, it won't be the last time I waste my time . . . Now the business is over and done with, how about finding a bar and having a drink or two to keep out the cold?'

'I do not drink alcohol.'

Was there a flight back to the island that night? wondered Alvarez.

It was five past five on Friday afternoon and there was a long silence over the telephone before Superior Chief Salas said: 'I confess that it had seemed to me as if there could be no further room for you to be wrong in what was, originally, a straightforward case. I should have remembered that in some respects you are a man of great ingenuity.'

'Señor, I . . .'

'However, even your ingenuity must finally be exhausted. So I would be exceedingly grateful if you'd now be kind enough to arrest the murderer of those two unfortunate persons,' said Superior Chief Salas, with insulting politeness. He rang off.

Alvarez slumped back in the chair. It was so very easy to be sarcastic and to point out that the identity of the murderer was obvious. Of course it was – now. If Charles Brent hadn't murdered Freeman and Mabel Cannon, Anson had. Despite his appearance of being a man who was above all direct, clearly his mind was tortuously clever. He had learned about the tontine and the death of Brent and he had realized that only two deaths lay between Caroline and a fortune. So he had taken those two lives.

It was going to be difficult to convince Caroline because women knew blind loyalties once their emotions were involved. But convinced she would eventually have to be, once told all the facts. Of course, she would hate him for being the person who exposed Anson, but perhaps eventually she would come to realize that he had only been doing his job and therefore her hatred was unjust.

He sighed, then stood up and left. He went down to his car and drove to the Port and the western arm of the harbour. There was a keen east wind coming between the headlands and across the bay and in the first impact of its chill he remembered the cold rain of the previous night and the commissaire who had looked down his nose at a dumb peasant from Mallorca. Well, he had been pretty dumb in many ways.

Mena was in the main shed, working on a traditionally shaped fishing-boat and helping two other men to position one of the ribs. Alvarez stood just beyond the skeleton shape which, when it was completed, would be a boat that was clearly utilitarian yet which nevertheless would have a simple beauty of line. 'Is the Englishman around?'

'He's out on the hard, trying to remove the screw of a pig of a French boat.'

'I'll go out and have a word with him . . . How did the wedding go?'

'Wonderful! The women wept all day, the men got tight, and the bridegroom fell and twisted his ankle.'

'If that's all he twisted, he'll be all right.'

The two other men sniggered.

Mena turned and spoke scornfully to one of them. 'You've no room to laugh. I've heard that when you got married, Carmen locked the bedroom door on you, you were so pickled.'

'Right enough, but only after I was on the inside.'

Mena spoke to Alvarez. 'Tell him if he still can't get

that screw off to hit the bloody thing with a five-kilo hammer and if anything breaks we'll charge the Frenchman double for all the trouble . . . And come and have a drink when you've finished with him.'

'I don't think I will, thanks.'

'Great God!' exclaimed Mena.

Alvarez passed a power boat whose 120 h.p. Mercury outboard lay in a cradle and left the shed through one of the side doors.

Anson, sweating, his face and hands stained with dirty grease, wearing a pair of filthy overalls, had just succeeded in removing the screw from the shaft. He stared belligerently at Alvarez.

'I want another word with you.'

'What about?'

The wind gusted and a sheet of newspaper scurried along the ground to wrap itself about Alvarez's feet. He shivered. 'Where can we go that's warmer than here?'

'You'd find it warm enough if you were working.' Anson waited, perplexed by the lack of any signs of irritation on the detective's part. He shrugged his shoulders and led the way into the main shed and across to a small office.

The room was small, overcrowded with a variety of things which clearly could be found no other home, and it smelled of tar and paint. There was a little furniture: a desk, covered with boat equipment, two chairs, one with a small winch on it, and an old and battered bookcase filled with tattered-looking books. Anson picked up the winch and cleared a space for it on the desk.

'Señor,' said Alvarez, once seated, 'as you know I am investigating the deaths of Señor Freeman and Señorita Cannon. I have before asked you questions and now I have some more to ask.'

'Go ahead. I can't stop you wasting your time.'

'Have you visited Cala San Pedro inside the last year?'

'I don't even know where it is.'

'On the Peninsula, in Rosas Bay.'

'I haven't been off the island in eighteen months.'

'Have you ever known a man called either Charles Brent or Peter Shore?'

'No. And what can any of this have to do with the deaths?'

'It has much to do with the señorita's wealth. Because Señor Brent died and then Señor Freeman, Señorita Cannon became possessed of a great deal of money. Now she has died and in her will she names Señorita Durrel. Did you know Señorita Cannon was very wealthy?'

'I've told you before – she obviously wasn't starving or she wouldn't have talked about lending me a million and a half, but more than that I've no idea.'

'Then it will surprise you for me to say she has wealth of more than twenty-five million pesetas?'

Anson stared at him, his expression one of wide amazement. 'Twenty-five million? Come off it! Someone's taking you for a sucker.'

'Let me assure you, she has more than that: how much more I do not yet know.'

'But twenty-five million . . . Carrie's going to have that much . . .' He suddenly swore.

'You seem worried, señor?'

'Of course I bloody am. If it had been going to be three or four million, that was great. But twenty-five million . . .'

'It becomes a very handsome dowry.'

'Not for me, it doesn't. You can guess what I'm worth. I've my hands and brains and a few years' experience of kicking around the world and being kicked by it. So if I meet a girl with nothing, we're level-pegging. If she's got a bit, that's fine, because it makes some things easier. But if she's got a fortune . . . I'm no gigolo.'

'A very proper sentiment,' said Alvarez, jealously knowing that implied in Anson's words had been a declaration of his love for Caroline.

'Sneer your head off.'

'Señor, I was not sneering. A man must be independent when he marries in order for his wife to respect him and a wife must respect or she becomes too sharp.' If Anson had wanted to play the scene in the way most complimentary to himself, thought Alvarez, this was surely how he would have played it – building up the picture of the fiercely independent suitor who positively resented the news that the woman he loved was rich. 'Señor, perhaps I can help you to feel less disturbed in this matter!'

'What d'you mean?'

'Although Señorita Cannon's estate will be possessed of more than twenty-five million, it is probably not hers so that it will be lost.'

'But you've just said . . .'

'It is money which was stolen in England and therefore must soon be returned.'

'You reckon she'd have anything to do with stolen money? You're round the twist.'

'It was like this. She was in love with Señor Freeman when they worked together in England and so Señor Freeman could persuade her to rob their firm. They stole almost a quarter of a million pounds. But as it is stolen money, it cannot remain. So Señorita Durrell will not be rich.' He watched, searching Anson's expression for the slightest hint of anger or despair, but saw only a puzzlement which appeared to be quite genuine. 'Señor, I will ask you again about all that happened when you visited Señorita Cannon on the day she died.'

Anson's expression became bitter. 'You can't stop hoping to prove I poisoned her, can you? Why have you got your knife into me? I suppose you hate the guts of all us foreigners?'

'I have no special feeling for foreigners,' said Alvarez, and he sounded pompous, 'and I speak to them as I speak to any Mallorquin . . . Señor, you will tell me what happened that evening.'

Anson spoke sullenly. 'I borrowed a cycle and went up to see her because Ramón was pressing me hard and I was a bloody fool and thought that on my own I could persuade her to lend me the money right away. I was prepared to offer her ten per cent interest on the money, more than she would have got from any of the local banks.'

'And were you not also prepared to offer a vision?'

Anson stared at him for a second or two, then slowly shook his head. 'I'm damned if I can begin to understand you. One moment you're like someone prejudiced blind, the next you sound as if you can really understand.'

'Please continue.'

'There's nothing to continue about. She obviously was spitting tacks in all directions, I was too thick to clear off and instead insisted on talking to her. Pretty soon, she got personal and told me she wouldn't lend a peseta to a boat-bum like me.'

'If I understand you, señor, you would not let her speak like that and say nothing yourself?'

'I've told you I'm no good at turning the other cheek.'

'So what exactly did you say to her?'

Anson became uneasy, even diffident. 'Look . . . I was all on edge because everything depended on her lending me the money. And she started calling me a boat-bum, a good-for-nothing layabout who'd use any money she was fool enough to give me to booze. Spend it on booze? I'd become TT for ten years if that'd help to get the partnership.'

'You still have not told me what you said to her?'

'I told her she was a dried-up prune and she wasn't

shocked when she caught Geoffrey tupping some blonde, she was jealous . . . All right, that makes me a real shit. The poor old cow couldn't help what she was like. But she'd cut pretty deep with her words and I wasn't trying to be nice.'

'And that was when she threw the paperweight?'

'And she'd have chucked anything else handy if she hadn't started to sneeze like she was about to blow up. So she stood there, sneezing, tears pouring down her cheeks and her nose streaming and I suddenly thought, You poor old cow, you never stood a chance, but you couldn't realize it. Matter of fact, I'd got to feel so sorry for her I even asked if there was something I could do. Between sneezes she shouted at me that there was – I could drop dead. So I cleared out.'

'You must have understood that now there was no chance for that loan?'

'Of course. But my mouth had always been bigger than my brains.'

'I wonder, señor, if you do not speak too poorly about your brains? After all, Señorita Cannon would not now lend you the money, but if she were dead and Señorita Durrel had all the money, then once more you could have the loan – even a gift, perhaps.'

'How often do I have to spell it out? I didn't know Carrie was going to get the money, I didn't know anything about the twenty-five million. All I did that night was bike back to the Port and get stinking tight.'

For several moments Alvarez stared out through the window which looked on to the harbour arm, then he stood up.

'Now what?' demanded Anson.

'I will leave you, señor, to finish your work.'

'Then you . . . you believe me.'

'I have carefully listened to all you have said.' He left,

ignoring a last question put to him, and walked through the shed, shouting goodbye to Mena on his way.

In his car, he sat behind the wheel, but did not immediately start the engine. It seemed to fit. Anson had needed the money quickly because Mena had set a deadline, but although this had been virtually promised, Mabel Cannon had become too mentally upset to give the loan. So Anson, who had learned about the tontine, had poisoned her . . . Yet Anson had appeared to be first genuinely astonished by the size of Mabel Cannon's fortune, then horrified by it because he could never see himself marrying a rich woman. Astonishment and horror could be simulated by a good actor, but could anyone as direct and aggressive in character as Anson be that good an actor? And how could he have originally learned about Geoffrey Freeman's passion for esclatasangs and have known he was going to eat them that first Thursday night? Or had Anson had nothing to do with Freeman's death and had he believed Mabel Cannon owned only the house and a small income so that Caroline Durrel would be able to give him the million and a half, yet would not be a rich woman? . . . But then who had murdered Freeman . . . ?

CHAPTER XX

Dolores stared across the table at Alvarez. 'The wind is pretty sharp again today. You really ought to wear a woollen vest.'

'Yes,' agreed Alvarez. He began to eat the hot soup.

'And don't forget to take your thicker coat.'

'Sure.'

'Enrique, what's the matter with you this morning?'

she asked, her voice troubled.

He looked up. 'Why should anything be?'

'Most days I try to look after you and see you stay healthy and you – who are as stubborn as the one-eyed mule my father worked – laugh at me. Today, you're just quietly agreeing with everything I say.'

'The truth is, I'm worried.'

'Ah! I knew there was trouble. What's the matter? Are you feeling ill? I'll make some tansy tea . . .'

'I'm fine. No, it's the case I'm working on. Every time I solve it, something happens to unsolve it. Superior Chief Salas is doing his nut.'

'That popinjay! What does he know about anything? If he isn't satisfied with the way things are done on this island, why doesn't he go back to Madrid?'

He finished the soup and pushed the bowl to one side. 'I'll tell you, though, he's got me wondering whether I'm not too old for the job.' But not too old to make a complete fool of himself over a beautiful young lady.

After she'd left the room, he ate. He cleared up the plates and carried them through to the kitchen. When he said goodbye to Dolores she asked him if he'd put on his woollen vest and he said he had. She called him a poor liar, but kissed him on both cheeks and hugged him as if he were leaving for a round-the-world voyage.

On the desk in his office were four letters. One of them had printed on the outside of the envelope, 'Institute of Forensic Anatomy'. He opened it and read the enclosed report. Señorita Mabel Cannon had died from a large dose of colchicine, distilled from colchicum seed. Colchicine was a cytotoxin, or cell poison, whose action was very similar to that of arsenic. It was sometimes, if mistakenly, called vegetable arsenic because it was the active principle of Autumn Crocus. 20 milligrams was considered a fatal dose (5 grams of colchicum seed).

He stared at the report and began to remember certain facts which could be correlated with other facts and as he did so he slowly began to suffer a bitter self-contempt.

After a while, he stood up. He sighed. God in His wisdom had made man weak, but why had He made him quite so weak?

He left and drove out to Casa Elba and after letting himself into the place and opening the shutters over the windows in the sitting-room, he crossed to the bookcase and picked out the book on vegetable poisons. Superior Chief Salas had been right to call him a fool. The important facts had been staring him in the face, yet he had allowed himself to be blinded by unimportant ones. A man of any intelligence would have distinguished between them right from the beginning.

He opened the book and searched the index for colchicine. He turned to page sixty-one and half-way down found the first pertinent reference. An attractive, colourful flower, *Colchicum autumnale* grew in profusion, sometimes carpeting a field. The poison was present in flowers, seeds, corm, and leaves, the last being visible only in the spring. Children often played with the seed pods. The toxic principle in the flower had long been known as a remedy, when used in therapeutic doses, for gout . . .

He turned the page. And there, bedded into the paper so that it did not fall even while he held the book at forty-five degrees, was a small, blackish seed. Very carefully, he put the book on a table and looked around for something into which to put the seed. Seeing nothing, he went down the passage and into the first of the two bathrooms and in a medicine cupboard there was an empty plastic medicine phial and some cotton wool. Back in the sitting-room, he carefully scooped the seed into the plastic phial and wedged it with cotton wool.

He resumed reading. Symptoms of poisoning appeared

a few hours, or in rarer cases days, after taking the poison. Burning throat and mouth, acute thirst, explosive vomiting, agonizing colics, paralysis of the central nervous system, great difficulty in breathing, and death from respiratory paralysis unless there was an intervening circulatory collapse. There was one final comment. 'The effects of this vegetable poison are so dramatic, so violent, so appalling, that they have to be witnessed before it can be fully appreciated what terrifying agonies can lie in plants which we so commonly know and, in the case of the Meadow Saffron, love for their attractive colours.'

He looked down at the phial and the seed which was just visible as a small black blob. Something that ordinary and insignificant could kill so hideously: it reduced a man to nearly nothing. He shut the book.

There was no cocktail cabinet, but there was a carved wooden chest against the wall. He went over to it and lifted the lid to find that it was indeed filled with bottles. He picked out a bottle of brandy, went through to the kitchen for a glass, and poured himself a very strong drink. God knows, he needed it! How could man believe in his eventual immortality when the seeds of a mere plant could crucify him in this life?

He had a second brandy. He should have remembered that if man was heir to nothing else, he was heir to his own emotions. When a peasant's land was threatened, he knew scorching hatred, when his animals were dying, he knew freezing despair. At heart, Mabel Cannon had been a peasant. A tall, juiceless, frustrated peasant woman, aching to release the heat in her loins, yet forever denied the opportunity. She had loved Geoffrey Freeman sufficiently to commit theft at his behest, even though but for love she would not have stolen a peseta from a millionaire. He had bribed her with the promise of love and then, when the theft was accomplished, he had refused to pay the bribe with callous indifference to her suffering.

Women, especially those with unfulfilled passions, had an astonishing capacity for suffering: perhaps they were essentially masochistically inclined. Mabel Cannon had gone on loving even knowing her love was mocked and had gone on hoping even knowing there could be no hope. That was, until the day she walked in and saw Veronica and Freeman.

Had she known before what passion really meant? Had she just dreamed, or had she shamefacedly sought details from books, photographs, and films? When she saw flesh in heat, had she experienced exaltation or revulsion?

From that moment on she was no longer able to live within her own delusions and so love somersaulted into hate. He had seduced her honour while refusing to seduce her body, he had mocked her, and he had betrayed her . . . So he must be punished.

She knew he had a passion for esclatasangs, she knew where to find the llargsomi which grew with them. Had she meant to kill or only to make him ill? Surely, only to make him ill. Because then she would have the chance to help nurse him back to health and enjoy the self-sacrifice involved in nursing her betrayer. But she had failed to appreciate the warning implicit in the description of the llargsomi. Its degree of toxicity depended on the victim. Geoffrey Freeman had been unusually susceptible and so he had died in agony.

Now it was necessary to see the world as she had seen it. She had murdered him cruelly, caused him physical agonies beyond description. She experienced self-hatred, despair, and wild remorse. One evening, Edward Anson had come to her house. He was rough and wholly masculine and he had shouted at her that she was too dried-up for any man ever to want. Hatred and the pains of frustration bore down on her self-hatred, despair, and remorse and suddenly, in the turmoil of her emotions, she realized something that should have been obvious long before. If she died, suffering agonies as great as Freeman had endured, she might find atonement. If the flesh were to be sufficiently tortured, surely the soul was released . . . ?

The facts had all been there, but he had overlooked them or else refused to acknowledge them from the moment he had learned about the money. He had believed the murderer must be pursuing a fortune whereas the murderer had been indifferent to the fortune. That money had been an irrelevance.

He poured himself another drink. Mabel Cannon had played a sad, thwarted, tragic part. But what part had he played? Had he truly believed money was the sole motive for the murder or had he merely needed self-justification for pursuing Edward Anson? Mabel Cannon had sinned, but in her madness her sins were forgivable. He had sinned but in his sanity his surely were not?

He finished his drink and then took his glass through to the kitchen, washed it, and put it on the rack to dry. He returned to the sitting-room and picked up the plastic phial and put it in his pocket, replaced the book of poisons in the bookcase, and left, locking the door after himself.

When he drove into Llueso he crossed the bridge and then bore right instead of going straight on and when he came to the following turning off to the left he braked to a halt. A car came up behind and hooted, but he ignored it and eventually it pulled out to pass. The driver shouted something at him which he failed to catch. He stared up the sloping road. Last time, he had promised himself never again.

He turned right and parked in front of the house with dark green shutters. As he climbed out, two boys, perhaps ten years old, pointed at him and laughed. Laugh now, he thought, but in seven or eight years' time you'll discover it's no laughing matter.

He knocked on the door and it was opened by Beatriz. She was dressed modestly and had on only discreet make-up. 'Enrique! . . . Come on in. It's ages and ages since you've been to see me.' She closed the door and kissed him chastely on both cheeks. 'Why have you been deserting me? For weeks I've been saying to myself, where is Enrique, why doesn't he come and see me any more?'

He mumbled some excuse about being so busy at work.

'You look tired. Or ill. Enrique, are you ill?'

He shook his head.

'But something's the matter with you.'

'I'm sick of myself. And I've been drinking much too much.'

'Haven't you always?'

She led the way into the sitting-room and while he sat on the settee, leaned his head back, and closed his eyes, she opened the right-hand door of an inlaid cabinet and brought out of it a bottle, two glasses, and a silver tray. She put the tray on the table, then sat beside him. 'No, don't open your eyes. I'm going to put a glass in your hand and afterwards I'll stroke your forehead and chase away all your stupid worries.'

She gave him a glass. She ran her fingertips across his forehead and he began to drift away from the troubled world. She whispered words of love and he believed them even while he was certain she must whisper such words to many men. Her lips closed on his and he put the glass down, brandy untouched, and gripped her and in her warmth and womanhood he found both physical and mental release.

'Father, I have sinned.

'I have loved a young and innocent woman. It's not

that I've ever touched her . . . Look, I'm no good at explaining things. I'm a simple, uneducated man and I can't make words mean what I want them to. But when I met her it was like meeting again my fiancée who was killed before we could be married. And I fell in love with this woman even though I'm twice her age and she's so beautiful that the devil himself wouldn't dare harm her. Because I loved her, I persecuted a man.

'I'm a police officer, sworn to uphold justice, yet I persuaded myself that he was responsible for a crime and closed my mind to all the evidence which could have told me he wasn't. I went out of my way to persecute him. I was trying to punish him because he was in love with her.

'And because I was so ashamed of what I'd done, I visited a woman I'd known before and had carnal knowledge of her . . . But you must understand that she's not the kind of person you'll imagine. She's kind and warm and . . .'

Alvarez left the church, a somewhat uneasy mixture of primitive baroque with brooding darkness and patches of over-bright colour, and he walked along one of the echoing passages of the monastery to the main doors and down the steps to the oblong courtyard. On his left was the shop, selling postcards and religious mementoes from which came the sound of taped music, and the medieval rest cells for travellers along a gallery, while on his right was a café: here, the sacred and the profane co-existed. Why should they not also co-exist in one troubled man?

His car was in the covered car-park, but he did not immediately go to it. Instead, he turned and looked up at the hill beyond the monastery on which stood a tall, very simple steel crucifix. He wondered if the priest had really understood? Not that it would be the priest's fault if not. He knew he hadn't been able to explain very clearly why his sin had been so much more complicated than if it had been mere jealousy and lust. He had never been able to define justice, but he had always been able to define injustice because it hurt. Yet he had been ready, eager, to perpetrate an injustice: he, who believed that the greatest of all sins was deliberately to hurt another . . .

He continued up to his car and sat behind the wheel. Poor, poor Señorita Mabel Cannon. Justice called her a murderer, but would not a Presence all-knowing and therefore infinitely more humane understand that she was not truly a murderer, only a victim? He hoped so.

CHAPTER XXI

Alvarez was re-packing the single seed which he had found in the book in Casa Elba when a guard looked into the room. 'There's a gorgeous piece of tail downstairs who's demanding to speak to the dashing, handsome Inspector Alvarez.'

'Shove off and get lost.'

'Well if you don't want to entertain her, I'll stand in.'

'D'you mean there really is someone?'

'D'you think I'd call in here for the pleasure of your company?'

'Who is she?'

'How would I know? She can't talk Spanish. But give me ten minutes alone with her and forget the dictionaries.' He left.

Hurriedly, Alvarez packed in a last wad of cotton wool and screwed home the top of the container. He didn't understand the younger men. Nothing was sacred to them, not even innocence. He hurried towards the door, but when he was half-way across there was a quick knock on it and Caroline entered.

'I'm sorry, but I had to come and see you and I managed to get one of the men to show me which was your room.' She spoke breathlessly and it was obvious that she was very nervous. 'I hope you don't mind too much?'

'Of course I don't mind, señorita. Please come in and sit down.'

He watched her sit. She was warm and kind and apparently defenceless, yet when there was someone who needed defending she possessed a sense of loyalty which became steel-like. Juana-Maria had been like that: insult her and her eyes would fill with tears, insult someone she loved and her anger scorched.

'I . . . I've come to ask you about Teddy.'

He sat behind the desk. 'Señorita, I am afraid that at this moment I cannot tell you exactly . . .'

'You can say whether you still believe he murdered Mabel.'

'I am trying to explain, señorita, that there are some facts which have to be . . .'

'Can't you understand the kind of person he really is? He'd never poison a person, knowing the terrible agony they'd suffer. If . . . if he did kill anyone, it would be with his fists or something he grabbed hold of and because he'd lost his temper and didn't know what he was doing. I know he went back and saw Mabel on Thursday, but he's told you everything that happened when he saw her. Of course he shouldn't have said what he did, but . . .' She became silent, unable to find any real excuse for his behaviour.

'Señorita, even though some things I do not yet know for certain, I can say this. It all seemed so complicated and I made mistakes, but now when this has been to the forensic laboratory – ' he tapped the plastic phial – 'then I shall finally be sure.'

'But what's it all mean? Are you still so stupidly wrong

that you think he could have murdered Mabel?'

He had to answer her. 'No, señorita, I do not think that.'

'Thank God!' she murmured. She was motionless for a while, then she sat more upright in her chair. 'You shouldn't ever have suspected him. You ought to have been able to see he wasn't that kind of a person. Just because he's not rich and doesn't own a villa . . .'

'Señorita, such facts have nothing to do with it.' If she could guess the real reasons for his actions, he thought, she would know contempt for him, not anger. 'Please understand that I had to ask questions of everybody and it did not matter to me whether the person was rich or poor.'

'But at long last you know it wasn't Teddy who killed her?'

'Yes.'

'Then who was it?'

'Señorita, I believe no one killed her. She killed herself.'

'Mabel committed suicide?'

'Think, please, of all that happened. Someone added a llargsomi to the esclatasangs which Señor Freeman ate. Why? Who had cause to hate him that much?'

'The husband of one of the wives?' she suggested uncertainly.

'Many husbands may have hated him, but I do not think it was one of them. The señorita was very fond of Señor Freeman, was she not, so fond that she had helped him commit a big crime in England?'

'Ted told me you said that. I still can't believe it.'

He spoke with sudden embarrassment. 'A woman – or a man – can do strange and stupid things when in love. She helped him with the swindle because she was in love with him. They came to this island and here she saw him with many women, but always she told herself perhaps that it was just a friendship, no matter what people said. Then, one day, she made a bad mistake and arrived at his house when he was entertaining a lady and she saw . . . No longer could she believe her own lies about him. Her love became a hatred. But when a woman has loved a man, she can never hate him completely; always, there is a little hope left that one day he will truly repent and turn to her. So she decided to punish him, but never to kill him. If he were ill and she nursed him with all the self-sacrifice she longed to make, could he help returning her love?

'She did not understand the poison and there was a dreadful mistake and he died. Now, her despair was total. And in this terrible despair she could see only one way of expiation – to suffer unto death as he had suffered.'

'It's horrible,' she whispered.

'Señorita, life and death are often horrible.'

'But to know anyone could get like that . . .' She stopped.

He could find no words of consolation. Even she had to learn how the world really was.

After a while her expression calmed. She stood up and came forward and shook his hand. 'Thank you so much for telling me everything,' she said, with simple gratitude. He accompanied her to the door, along the corridor, and down the stairs to the street door, where they said good-bye. As he watched her walk along the street he could still feel the smooth presence of her hand on his: the first time he had touched her.

Caroline walked through the entrance of the boatyard and Mena, who had been standing by a car and talking to a couple, hurried over. 'Señorita Durrel, how go you?' he asked, in his laboured English. 'Eduardo is speak to a man. Come to drink.'

'It's a bit early . . .'

'Is never early,' he answered, with a gusto which Alvarez would have appreciated.

They went into Mena's office and he poured her out a large brandy and then, in a mixture of fractured English and Spanish, flirted with her with the breezy humour of a man who was too old and sensible to be dangerous, yet not so old he didn't have ideas.

He had left a message for Anson to come to the office, but when Anson arrived it was clear he had not been told that Caroline was there. He stared at her with considerable astonishment. 'What's brought you here?'

'There's something I had to tell you.' She tried to speak casually, but could not hide her excitement.

Mena smiled at her. 'I will go and see everyone is working and not sitting around and wasting my money,' he said, in Spanish. He drained his glass and put it down on the desk, stood up and walked to the door. As he passed Anson, he winked. 'There is no hurry. And help yourself to a drink.' He left, shutting the door behind himself.

'He's rather nice, isn't he?' she said.

'Sure, provided you're not trying to do business with him . . . What have you come to tell me?'

'I've just been to see the detective, Teddy. I went along to where he works and asked him if he was still so silly as to believe you'd poisoned Mabel.'

Anson stared at her for a while, then poured himself out a drink. 'I reckon I need this.' He drank. 'Carrie, didn't anyone explain to you that you don't ever speak to a Spanish policeman like that?'

'Why not? He didn't mind.'

He shook his head. Then, his manner became once more worried. 'So what was the answer?'

'He told me he wasn't being stupid any longer. Mabel committed suicide. She wanted to hurt Geoffrey because of what she'd seen in his house, but made a terrible mistake because although she'd only meant to make him ill, the llargsomi she put with the esclatasangs killed him. She was so shocked and upset that in the end she committed suicide.'

He walked over to the window and stared out. 'Poor old Mabel. She just couldn't get a single thing right.'

'I keep thinking of how frightfully she suffered . . .'

He turned back and his voice sharpened. 'Forget it. You did everything you could for her, unlike most of them round here who just thought her finding him wrapped round another woman was funny . . . Look forward, Carrie, not backwards. Grab life by its head, not its tail.'

'All right. I'll start looking forward. What about us?'

'How d'you mean?'

'Teddy, now you're being thick.'

He became uneasy. 'Look, I'd better get back to work because . . .'

'What have I got to do, then? Wait until leap year?'

'Carrie, I . . . I've got nothing.' He jammed his hands into his pockets. 'Not even a bloody spare peseta to throw at the wind.'

'And that's important?'

'Of course it is.'

'Aren't you being incredibly old-fashioned? I thought these days everyone had learned to be much more sensible about things. In any case, how can you say you've nothing? You've your skill, your enthusiasm, and your ambition. And I've the money. So we just put them together . . .'

'Didn't the detective explain to you?'

'Explain what?'

'That it seems all the money Mabel and Geoffrey had came from the swindle they carried out back in England? So the money in their estates will all be claimed back.'

'Oh! . . . So I'm not rich after all?'

'No.'

She thought for a while, then smiled. 'Now I understand. You're not interested in me any longer because I'm poor instead of being rich?'

He strode up to the desk, took his hands from his pockets and thumped them down on the top. 'How in the hell can you say that? God Almighty, do I have to spell it out for you?'

'Yes, please.'

He stared at her with longing. 'I loved you the first time I saw you, Carrie. Just like all the fairy stories you've always believed in and I never have. But I was a boat-bum and you were the beautiful princess. You didn't patronize me, or cut me, or treat me like the social undesirable so many of the others reckon me because I work with my hands, and like a fool I began to dream. I dreamt that there'd be a miracle and I'd find a job that would pay enough for me to be able to ask you to marry me. And you'd say yes and we'd live happily ever after. But I knew it was a dream. Then Mena offered me the partnership and it seemed perhaps it could be more than a dream . . . It became a nightmare. The detective thought I'd killed Mabel for her money . . . But now . . .'

'But now?' she repeated softly.

'Now I'm right back at the beginning. The nightmare's gone, but so has the dream. I can't take the partnership because I haven't the money and there's no way of finding it.'

'If only you'll offer him as much as I can rake up . . .'

'I'm not taking a penny from you of your own money.'

'That's being stupidly stubborn.'

'Perhaps. But that's the way it's going to be.'

'Then how are you going to get the partnership?'

'I've just told you. I'm not.'

'Teddy,' she said softly, 'do you know something very strange about us?'

'What?'

'You've never even kissed me, you damn fool.'

'I . . . I've been too scared to.'

'You, scared? I don't believe you're scared of anything or anyone.'

'I'm scared of myself.'

'Well, I'm not. So come here.'

He went.

The report from the forensic laboratory arrived in the afternoon, having been brought from Palma on the bus. The seed was identified as the seed of *Colchicum autumnale*, or Meadow Saffron. All such seed contained the poison colchicine.

Alvarez leaned back in his chair and wondered, yet again, what the señorita had thought as she swallowed the poison? And had she found redemption in the agony, or had that been so great that before she died she couldn't understand her own madness?

He was going to have to telephone Superior Chief Salas now and explain that all his previous reports on the case were incorrect.

There were days when the winter weather was as fine as travel agents would have it always and Saturday was one such. The sun was hot, the sky was cloudless, the air was sparkling, and it could have been early May.

Alvarez walked into the Club Llueso and entered the bar.

'Hullo, stranger,' said the barman. 'Haven't seen you in here for so long I thought you must have been posted.'

'I've been hell's bells busy.'

'You want to watch it, you know – too much work is

bad for the liver. What'll it be, then? The usual?'

'Make it a large one.' He yawned. 'Thank God to-morrow's Sunday and I can rest.'

'Some people are born lucky. Me? I'll be working here.'

'My heart bleeds for you, so have a drink with me?'

'Are you paying for it?'

'I suppose. I'm just too soft-hearted.'

The barman poured out two brandies. As he pushed one glass across the bar, he looked past Alvarez and saw a priest enter. 'Hullo, it looks as if you're wanted, Enrique,' he said in a low voice.

Alvarez turned. Father Farras was a five-foot button of a man, with a face which looked old and simple, who had the strength of a giant when he was wrestling with Satan.

'Enrique,' said Father Farras, his voice expressing a certain annoyance, 'when I saw you crossing the square I shouted and shouted, but you never stopped.'

'I'm sorry, Father. I was in a bit of a hurry.'

'Quite so!' Father Farras looked at the glass in Alvarez's hand.

'It's my first today. Or very nearly, anyway. Would you like one?'

'I normally never indulge, as you know, but since I'm actually in a bar . . .' Father Farras leaned forward to speak to the barman. 'A small, a very small, coñac, please.'

The barman poured out a large brandy and passed the glass across. Father Farras drank with evident pleasure and when he'd emptied his glass, which he did slightly before Alvarez emptied his, he said: 'Enrique, I want to have a word with you, so we can walk back together.'

'I'm afraid I'm very busy . . .'

'But certainly not too busy to give me just a few of your very valuable minutes of time.'

Alvarez sighed, but accepted that there was no way of escape. He paid for the drinks and followed Father Farras out of the club.

Father Farras, to compensate for his lack of height, walked with hurried steps and so anyone accompanying him had to hurry to keep pace: upon which, as if the sight of someone hurrying galvanized him to even greater efforts, he would increase his own pace. A walk with him usually ended up as a race.

Alvarez automatically half-turned to make for the steps leading up to the raised part of the square.

'No, Enrique, we will go right round because I wish to ask you about certain matters.' He nodded and smiled at a man who was passing, acknowledged a woman with a baby, and waved at two young children who were roller-skating. He seldom did only one thing at a time. He turned and spoke over his left shoulder. 'I have known you for a great number of years, have I not?'

'I suppose it is rather a long time,' replied Alvarez, already beginning to be short of breath.

'I remember that at your first communion you giggled rather a lot, probably because you failed to understand the true meaning of the ceremony.'

'When one's young . . .' began Alvarez.

'Since then I have watched you grow up and I have tried, not always successfully, to guide you through the shocks of life and to help you in times of trouble. That is so, is it not?'

Alvarez felt sweat break out on his forehead.

Father Farras swept across the road, immediately in front of a car which had to brake sharply. He increased his rate of walking as Alvarez drew level with him. 'Until now I have therefore felt that between us is a spiritual bond. Do I make myself clear?' He skipped to one side to avoid hitting a pram, stopped abruptly to cluck the baby under the chin, then charged forward to surge past Alvarez who had come to a halt. 'Do you understand me?' he demanded loudly, not bothering to turn his head.

'The devil I do,' muttered Alvarez, as he began to breathe through opened mouth.

'I want you to understand one thing. In no way do I speak from a sense of ingratitude. There is no place for ingratitude, or gratitude, between a priest and his flock. No, what lies within me is a feeling of . . .' He stopped to stare at a display of girlie magazines in the window of a small newsagent. He opened the door and put his head inside. 'Juana, the window is no place for magazines such as you've put there. If you have to stock such abominations, keep them inside and out of sight and so force men to question their consciences as well as you before they can buy them.' He did not wait for any comment, but skipped away. 'I speak from a sense of bewilderment. Where have I failed?'

'Failed what?' gasped Alvarez.

Father Farras stopped. He stared critically up at Alvarez. 'You're in very bad physical shape. You must eat less and drink a very great deal less.'

Alvarez took a handkerchief from his pocket and mopped his face.

'Body and soul are entwined,' said Father Farras, rushing forward. 'Neglect one and inevitably the other suffers.' He turned left and bolted past the main entrance to the church.

It was all very well to talk about cutting down on food and drink, thought Alvarez, but it would surely have been more to the point to slow down the rate of progress.

'Come on . . . Where have I failed you, Enrique? How have I inadvertently failed to maintain that spiritual bond?'

'But I don't know what you're talking about.'

'You puff along there, man and giggling boy, and tell me you don't know? Did you, or did you not, attend a church on Sunday?'

'Yes, I did.'

'And there you made confession?'

'Well, yes. You see . . .'

'Since your first communion, you have confessed in my church. And I have struggled to help you in your times of need – which have occurred rather frequently. Yet now you attend another church! How do you imagine that reflects on me?' He stopped and looked up, his head tilted on one side and his eyes sharply bright.

Alvarez tried to regain his breath.

'Not that it is from any sense of hurt pride that I speak out. I am concerned solely with your soul. After all, can anyone doubt that a pastor to a soul for many, many years is more likely to be able to bring comfort to such a soul than someone who meets it for the first time?'

'I just happened to be up in the mountains last Sunday and . . .'

'You always were a bad liar,' said Father Farras sadly.

Alvarez mopped the sweat from his face again as he tried, and failed, to appear less like a small boy caught scrumping apples. He had been a fool to think for one moment that he could confess in another church on the island without Father Farras getting to hear about it. And having heard, Father Farras had every right to be annoyed. How would a farmer feel who had sold cabbages to his neighbour for forty years only to have them refused as inedible in the forty-first? 'I was too ashamed to confess my sins to someone who knew me personally,' he mumbled.

Father Farras stared critically at him. 'Enrique, can you be quite certain you are free from the sin of boastful pride? I can remember that when you were a giggling

boy you were rather inclined to exaggerate for effect.'
He bounded forward and rushed up the rising road, past
the creepered wall of the church. 'I must not now, of
course, enquire into the nature of your sins . . .' He was
silent for half a dozen paces. When Alvarez said nothing,
he frowned briefly. 'But I feel constrained to point out
that the orthodoxy of the Monastery of Laraix has
always been suspect . . . Well, that's that, then.' He came
to a halt. 'We'll say no more about it and forget the
matter, once and for all. How is your cousin and her
family?'

'They're all fine. Isabel is doing well at school – she got
two excellents . . .'

'I do not remember having seen either her or Juan
recently amongst the congregation . . . But then you, of
course, have not been free to bring them since you have
been treading the paths of unorthodoxy.'

'It's not that. I've been working flat out, trying to solve
the deaths of the two English.'

'Ah, yes! Terrible, terrible, for the señor to die in an
unfortunate faith. And do you now know who killed
them?'

'The first death was accidental in that the woman
meant only to hurt, not to kill. The second death was
suicide.'

'Señorita Cannon committed suicide?'

'That's right. She was so overwhelmed by the horror of
what she'd done she felt she could only expiate her sin by
committing suicide and suffering as much as she had made
him suffer.'

'Ha!' exclaimed Father Farras. 'Perhaps you know
everything about detection, but you know nothing about
the souls of people. Suicide! Balderdash! Some months
ago the señorita came to me for spiritual advice. Though
of our faith, she had not visited my church because of

something which had happened in England. Desperate in her misery, she came to me for help and I led her to understand something which she should clearly have remembered – none of us (remember this in your pride) is beyond redemption if there is true repentance. She rejoiced when she understood. Yet you stand there, panting and sweating because you drink and eat too much, and you try to tell me that she would have damned her soul by committing suicide? . . . Stick to your last and leave others to interpret the soul.' He waved both hands in the air to emphasize his words. Then he saw someone he knew and wanted to speak to and he darted off, his short legs working like pistons.

CHAPTER XXII

Alvarez lay in bed and stared up at the ceiling, faintly picked out by the light which came through the closed shutters. What a night! Dream had followed dream and if he'd woken once, he'd woken half a dozen times. His mind had been on a monstrous roundabout which nothing would slow down.

No man was infallible. Not even an elderly, autocratic village priest who knew everything about everybody. So he could be wrong about Mabel Cannon. Her despair might have been so great that the future of her soul became of no consequence to herself. And yet . . . And yet, busy-body that he was, fifty years of priesthood must have given him an insight into people's souls which almost bordered on the sublime. So if he maintained that Mabel Cannon would never have committed suicide, then the proposition had to be considered with very great serious-ness.

But if she had not committed suicide, she had been murdered and who but Edward Anson would and could have murdered her?

He swore bitterly. To have to return to questioning Anson would be to have to return along paths he had hoped to leave forever behind himself. How would Caroline then look at him . . .?

He could just make out the bedside table and he reached over and picked up a cigarette, which he lit. Murder by poisoning presupposed a strong motive. Here, there had been two motives for killing Freeman, only one for killing Mabel Cannon. Had Anson poisoned her for her money, forgetting that the source of the tontine must almost inevitably come to light in the wake of the investigations so that the money would be lost to Caroline? Yet hadn't his uneasiness on learning about the extent of Caroline's apparent inheritance been genuine? Then he hadn't killed her for her money.

Father Farras had to be wrong. And having finally decided that, he once more tried to work out where *he* had gone wrong if Father Farras was right. And eventually he saw that he had not allowed for the impossible.

There was now no owner living in Ca'n Ritat to see that they did their job properly, yet Luis and Matilde Blanco continued to work as thoroughly as they had ever done. Beds not slept in were remade, rooms were dusted, carpets vacuumed, chairs polished, tiled floors washed . . .

Matilde was washing down the north wall of the kitchen when Alvarez arrived on the Tuesday morning.

'Hullo,' he said.

'Good morning, señor.'

'I've come here to ask you something.'

Immediately she was worried. 'I've told you all I know. I swear that I have . . .'

'There's no need to flap. All I want to find out is whether Señor Freeman said anything to you about lunch on Friday, the twenty-third of October, and did he have an appointments book or a calendar on which he noted down invitations?'

She looked perplexedly at him.

'Tell you what, how about starting off with a cup of coffee? Is that possible, even if the stuff does cost more than gold now?'

'Of course I can make coffee, señor. And maybe you would like a coñac in it?'

'Spoken like a true Christian.' He sat down at the table and watched her spoon coffee into an electrically operated espresso machine. 'D'you remember the day the señor had a friend called Veronica Milton here and Señorita Cannon arrived and walked into the house instead of waiting to see if it was safe to do so?'

She nodded and blushed.

'I'm interested in the next day. Can you think back to it? Did he tell you that Señorita Cannon was coming to lunch on the Friday and what kind of a meal he wanted?'

'No, señor.'

'Can you be quite sure of that?'

'Indeed. You see, the señorita did not like any rich food, but the señor did. He would have asked for two different dishes and I would certainly remember.'

A simple answer to a simple question, but what a complicated difference it made! 'I'm sure you remember exactly, señora, but in my job we have to check up on everything. Did the señor keep an appointments book?'

She filled a jug with milk so that the machine would warm it. 'He used to write things down on the calendar by the telephone, but they were in English so I didn't really understand them although some clearly were appointments.' Her tone of voice had suddenly become sharply disapproving.

'Where is the telephone?'

'In the hall.'

He stood up and went through into the hall. The telephone was on a small corner cupboard and by its side was a calendar and when he saw this he understood why she'd been so disapproving – there was half a month to a page and a pin-up to each half-month. All the previous pages had been retained and in the interests of a thorough investigation he went back to January 1 and studied each page. The second half of October was adorned by a red-head, noticeable for consistency. There were luncheon or drink appointments for every day but the twenty-second and the twenty-third. At the beginning those blanks would have had no special meaning for him, now he knew they held the answer to the riddle of the two deaths.

He returned to the kitchen.

'Did you find it?' she asked.

'I did, thanks. And checked right through it.'

She blushed as she smiled.

Blanco, dressed in overalls that were splattered with damp patches, came into the kitchen. 'I've been cleaning the pool,' he said after greeting Alvarez. 'And before that I washed the big car down. She's a beauty. If I had a million, I'd buy it.'

'And have all the luxury taxes to pay?'

'If I could afford a million for a car, why should luxury taxes bother me?' He undid the buttons and began to strip off the overalls.

'You've a point there. It must be strange to be rich and so not have to worry about where the next ten thousand pesetas are coming from.'

'If rich means being like him, I'd rather stay poor,' said Matilde.

'You've an even better point there,' agreed Alvarez.

The machine hissed as the coffee made. Matilde poured out three cupfuls, added milk to each and a liberal tot of brandy to two, then passed the cups round.

Blanco, who'd thrown his overalls on to the floor by the the side of the outside door, sat down at the table. He spooned sugar into his coffee. 'So you're still looking round the place?'

'Still looking,' agreed Alvarez.

'Then it's wrong what I was told – that you'd found out all what happened?'

'I'm afraid it was wrong – until now.'

'And now you know? So what did happen?'

Alvarez sipped the coffee. 'Señorita Cannon was so shocked and upset by what she saw here when she found him with Veronica that she put a llargsomi in with the esclatasangs he was going to eat that night. There's no proof of this, but I'm certain all she meant to do was to make him ill. She overdid things, though, and killed him.'

'And then she committed suicide?'

'No. She was murdered.'

'Who killed her?'

'Señor Freeman,' replied Alvarez. He picked up the cup and finished the coffee.

CHAPTER XXIII

He should, of course, have divined the truth almost from the beginning – but then although he had a certain peasant sharpness in some matters, he had never made the mistake of thinking of himself as intelligent.

He leaned over and opened the bottom drawer of his

desk and brought out the bottle of brandy and poured himself a generous drink.

Looking at things back to front, and it was that sort of a case, it was easy to see that his greatest mistake had been to accept the logic of the sequence of events. Freeman had died before Mabel Cannon and therefore logically there were only three possibilities: Mabel Cannon had killed Freeman and then committed suicide; she had killed him and in turn been killed by a third person; or a third person had killed both of them. Yet seen back to front there was a fourth possibility. Mabel Cannon had poisoned him and he had poisoned her – after he was dead.

He should have studied the motives together, instead of separately. Wherever there were large sums of money, there was motive for murder, wherever there were strong emotions, there was motive for murder. The tontine had been set up by the three of them, Freeman, Mabel Cannon, and Charles Brent. (Surely this must have been at Freeman's suggestion, ostensibly to avoid their having too much money available to spend which might have drawn attention to themselves, in fact because he had an eye firmly fixed on the main chance?) Each of them, after buying a house, had been drawing a very good income from the tontine, soon to be made even larger by the strength of the Swiss franc when compared with softer currencies. In April of this year, Freeman had passed fifteen million pesetas through his bank account in Palma which had not gone through his account in Puerto Llueso. Where had it gone and why had he had to draw it? Assume he had earlier been engaged in some sort of financial speculation which had gone sour, leaving him owing this large sum of money. Where was he going to get it from? There was more than enough left in his share in the tontine, but that capital could not be drawn without the written consent of the other two members and as the survivor took all it was not in their interests to allow him to withdraw so much. Mabel Cannon wouldn't have bothered where her interests lay because she was in love with him, but Brent would have objected. Being the younger man, Brent would have hopefully believed he was going to be the survivor who inherited all, little realizing the unlikelihood of this if Freeman had his way. So unless Brent's veto could be removed, there was no hope of Freeman withdrawing the money he needed. Brent had died in the middle of March and the cause of death had been recorded as accidental whilst drunk. But that must have been a carefully planned murder.

With Brent dead, Freeman could have had little difficulty in persuading Mabel Cannon to agree to his withdrawing fifteen million pesetas in Swiss francs from the tontine. And as everything had gone so smoothly with the first death, why not start thinking earlier than he would otherwise have done about the second one which would make the tontine wholly his? A thought which might well have been underlined if and when she began to talk about making restitution to their old firm. (She had sought spiritual guidance from Father Farras. The little priest, who never fought Satan with less than a full armament, would have insisted on that.)

Freeman could have killed her and made her death look like another accident, but he was a clever man, as proved by his successfully planned and executed swindle, and he realized that there was always the chance, however remote it might seem in times of optimism, that someone in authority would learn about the tontine and the 'accidental' deaths which had overtaken two of the members and would begin to investigate. So he decided she must appear to commit suicide.

She was very interested in the flora of the island and in her house was a book on poisons in plants. He read through

the book and chose colchicine. The motive for her suicide
was easily found. She loved him sufficiently to shut her
eyes to all his affairs. There's none so blind as they that
won't see. But what happens when you force a thirty-
nine-year-old spinster into seeing the truth in all its naked
passion?

He'd asked her to lunch at his house on the Thursday.
(Here he made a mistake – he didn't record the invitation
on his appointments calendar with the consistent red-
head.) On that day he met Veronica and took her back to
Ca'n Ritat and there, with one eye on the time wherever
the other eye was fixed, he began to make love to her in the
sitting-room. Would any man, experienced in affairs,
normally make love to a woman in the sitting-room,
knowing the servant might enter whatever she'd been told
to do? Veronica had protested, but he'd given her sufficient drink to make certain her protests weren't as strong
as they would otherwise have been. And sharp on time
(people like Mabel Cannon were always good time-
keepers, even in Mallorca) Mabel Cannon had come into
the sitting-room and seen them. A sight to shock and
torment a love-sick spinster.

His biggest mistake, of course, had been to under-
estimate Mabel Cannon's passion for him, presumably
because he had held her in contemptuous amusement. He
had never bargained for the depths of her shock or the
breadth of her torment. She planned a revenge that would
punish him for his wicked betrayal of her and yet at the
same time give her the chance to nurse him back to health
and so prove that her devotion would survive anything.
Her biggest mistake had been to fail to understand the
potency of the poisonous llargsomi.

So he died, but he had reached out from his grave to
murder her. Just prior to the carefully contrived love-
scene with Veronica which was to provide the motive for

suicide, he had emptied the contents of one of her anti-histamine pills and substituted colchicine. It was a fool-proof method of murder, suffering only the one disadvant-age that the time of her death must be haphazard. Yet if she died very soon after finding him *in flagrante delicto*, people would say the awful shock had tragically affected her, if she died many days afterwards they would say that she had been brooding over what had happened until she could no longer face the world.

She took the fatal pill after Anson visited her on the Thursday after Freeman died. Her hay fever had ob-viously been triggered off both by causative agents and by such agents combined with heightened emotions. And Anson, with typically blunt words, had upset her so badly that she'd had a bad attack. She took one of the pills and it contained the colchicine. If Freeman had not previously died, her death would almost certainly have been recorded as suicide, exactly as planned.

Alvarez poured himself another drink.

On the following Monday afternoon the head booking clerk in the Palma office of Iberia rang Alvarez. 'Regard-ing that call of yours. I've managed to trace out the flight you're interested in.'

'That's great. When was it?'

'Señor Freeman flew on the sixteenth of March.'

Brent had died on the eighteenth. 'When did he come back?'

'Three days later, on the nineteenth.'

It wasn't proof in the legal sense – perhaps the death of Brent now never could be proved to have been murder – but it was proof enough for him. He thanked the other and rang off. He stood up and crossed to the window and looked down at the street, rather dismal under the steady rain which had been falling since early morning. Almost all the loose ends were now tied up, but it occurred to him that he should bring the appointments calendar away from Ca'n Ritat because it provided one link in the chain. There was, he thought with satisfaction, a measure of morality in all that had taken place. Three people had carried out a swindle: these three had died because they had taken with them their greed and their passions.

He left his office and went downstairs and out to his car. He drove to the Llueso/Palma road, turned left, and as he passed the new school he wondered whether Juan was now working at his studies harder than he had been. If Isabel could get excellent, why couldn't he? The road rounded the outcrop of rock and he came in sight of the mountains. Because of the rain they were slate grey in colour and bleak in nature and they made him feel un-happy so that he was troubled by the thought of who would visit his grave when he was dead. Isabel and Juan? But the young today didn't observe the customs as their parents had. How many of them now spent All Souls' Day in the family cemetery? How many welcomed their aged parents (and uncles) into their homes when they were no longer capable of looking after themselves?

There was a car in the drive of Ca'n Ritat and when he parked behind it and looked into the courtyard he saw Caroline. Suddenly the day was no longer grey.

She was wearing a lightweight anorak with a hood that was pulled over her head, to make her look like a pixie. She was feeding the dog which looked round at Alvarez but did not bother to bark. When he entered the court-yard, she said: 'Hi, there! I'm just feeding Cheetah.'

'Lucky dog!' He watched her empty out a piece of meat from a plastic bag. The dog caught it and began noisily to eat.

'Mabel used to do this every Monday because it's the Blancos' day off. She was always so afraid that they wouldn't bother to feed him because . . . Oh!' Her expression became confused.

He smiled. 'No doubt, señorita, she did not believe any Mallorquin could be trusted to bother about a mere dog on his day off?'

'She was rather silly when it came to animals.'

'But you also must have a little doubt or you surely wouldn't bother to come here today?'

After a while she smiled ruefully at him. 'All right, you've caught me out fair and square. I did wonder whether they'd remember Cheetah and I couldn't bear to think of him going hungry so I bought a couple of lamb chops.'

'Whole lamb chops, señorita?'

'Yes.'

He would never begin to understand the English. Lamb chops cost so much that it made him incredulous just to look at the prices. But she had bought two for a dog which would have been better off with a lump of paunch.

She watched the dog swallow the last of the bone. 'There you are, Cheetah. At least you ought to have pleasant dreams tonight.' She pointed at the battered drum which was the kennel. 'That can't be watertight. Why don't people look after their dogs better out here? I mean, you see them chained up in fields with much worse shelter than this drum and so thin they're obviously half-starved and then there are all the strays with the most awful sores . . .' She stopped. She reached up and pushed the hood a little further back from her forehead. 'I'm terribly sorry, I shouldn't have criticized like that. After all, you're not like us – you don't need to have a society to prevent cruelty to children. But it so hurts to see animals suffering.'

'I think you are a person who hurts too easily.'

'I suppose so.' She sighed. 'Ted sometimes calls me a

naïve idealist who doesn't know how much ideals cost . . .
I often wonder where he read that.' She smiled once more.
'Now I'm being beastly to him. It's not my day, is it?'

'How is he?' he asked, not giving a damn.

'The same as ever,' she said, and there was now a
strained note in her voice.

He looked at the kitchen door. 'Let's go and see if we
can beg a cup of coffee to drive away the rain.'

'But they're out.'

'Of course.' He was irritated by his own stupidity. But
when he looked at her, more beautiful than a field of
wheat ready for harvest, he became stupid.

'I wish he weren't so terribly stubborn,' she said, breaking the silence.

She desperately wanted to talk about Anson, he thought.
And because every word she spoke would hurt and
because he had so many sins to try to expiate, he must
listen and suffer. 'Señorita, will you come and have coffee
with me in the village? It would be a very great pleasure
for me.'

'All right . . . I mean, I'd love to.'

If Anson had asked her, she'd have been thrilled. But
in the name of reason, why should she be thrilled when a
near-pot-bellied, middle-aged detective asked her? He
watched her pat the dog and promise that she would be
back next Monday, and tried not to think of the depths of
affection she would have for the man she loved. He went
with her to her car and held the driving door open and the
smile of thanks she gave him was like a knife.

In the square there were two empty parking places
adjoining and they drew into these. He saw her out of her
car and then led the way into the Club Llueso. The bartender looked at Caroline with obvious appreciation, but
when Alvarez glared at him he hastily assumed a blank
expression. Alvarez showed her to a table and then re-

turned to the bar. 'Two coffees.' He hesitated, then added: 'And two coñacs.'

He sat down opposite her, by a window which looked out on to the steps leading up to the raised section of the square. She opened her small leather handbag and brought out a pack of cigarettes, which she offered. Once her cigarette was alight, she said, a far-away look in her eyes: 'Teddy's so stubborn, I could kick him. I've argued and argued, but I might as well have saved my breath. And I used to think . . .'

'You used to think what, señorita?'

'I used to think he was really modern. But he's as old-fashioned and stick-in-the-mud as my grandmother's clock – which never worked.'

The barman brought over the coffees and the brandies.

'I thought that perhaps you would like a coñac with your coffee?' said Alvarez.

She nodded, but it was clear that she wasn't really paying any attention to what he said. 'I asked him who the hell worries about security these days? There isn't any for anyone. But he went on and on about how I must be so careful and how we'd have to wait and see what happens. There isn't the time to wait.'

He poured a brandy into his coffee, added a spoonful of sugar, and stirred.

'In the end I told him I'd just move in with him.'

A small fire of hate built up in Alvarez's mind.

'But he wouldn't hear of it because we aren't married. In this day and age! Half my married friends aren't married.'

He was shocked that she could talk like this.

She fiddled with her cigarette. 'He won't marry me because he hasn't any money and he won't get any money until he's a partner and he won't become a partner because he hasn't any money. He won't take what I've got and see if Ramón would credit him with the remainder, especially if I went and worked in the office to help with the paperwork. He won't live with me because he says we've got to be married first . . . I could brain the stubborn man.' She suddenly looked at Alvarez with surprise. 'I can't think why I'm talking to you like this, as if you were my favourite uncle.'

At least, he thought, she hadn't said her father. 'Sometimes, señorita, it is easier to talk about events that worry you to someone who is a stranger.'

'But you're not a stranger, you're a friend.'

'Señorita, you are very kind. It is a great honour to be your friend.'

She smiled warmly. 'I love the way all of you are so emotionally kind. If any islander can help someone who's in trouble, he will. I know for certain that if I came to you for help you'd give it to me, if you possibly could.'

'Of course.'

She sighed. 'If only I could.'

'Could what, señorita?'

'Ask you to knock some sense into his thick, thick skull,' she said fiercely, then laughed. 'Oh well, that's more than enough of all my troubles. I never used to bore everyone with them, so I can't think why I do now.' She drank, finishing her coffee. 'I suppose I'd better get moving because I said I'd call in and see Betty. The poor woman's fallen and broken her hip so she can't get around anywhere and not very many people are calling in to see her.'

He vainly wished he could find the words which would hold her, even for just a little longer.

'Goodbye,' she said, and stood up. He followed suit. 'I should have said, Until the next time, shouldn't I, not goodbye?' She smiled and left and her manner made it clear she did not want him to accompany her back to her car.

He sat down, looked at his empty cup, then at his smoking cigarette, which he stubbed out. 'Let's have the same again,' he called out to the bartender, 'but don't worry about the coffee this time.'

'One large coñac coming up.'

The barman brought the brandy to the table. 'A lovely woman . . .'

'She's a lady and you'd better not bloody well forget that.'

'Sure,' said the barman and, thinking that you could never really trust a policeman, he returned to the bar.

Alvarez drank and very soon his glass was empty. 'Bring me another,' he ordered.

'Are you sure, Enrique? It's still only the afternoon and the last time you got pissed in the afternoon you asked me never to . . .'

'I'm not asking, I'm telling you. Bring another large coñac.'

'One large coñac,' said the barman morosely.

Alvarez lit another cigarette and was hardly aware of the precise moment when the brandy was brought to the table, although after a while he reached down for the fresh glass and drank the contents. She didn't belong to the modern, hard, selfish world: she needed an age of soft elegance and wide compassion . . . Yet it had been she who had suggested an affair and Anson who had rejected the idea. How to understand that? How could she love Anson? He might have some qualities which one could eventually learn to admire, but he'd never have the wit or subtlety to appreciate her as completely as he should. Who could ever imagine him buying lamb chops to feed the dog because it was the Blancos' day off . . .?

Sweet Mary! he suddenly thought.

He looked at his empty glass. Was he drunk, so that his mind was a maze of nonsense? But since when had a mere three brandies affected him?

It was totally impossible! He couldn't still be wrong. But the dog *had* barked and howled. Monday *was* the Blancos' day off. Matilde had *not* cooked the supper even though it had been a Thursday . . .

CHAPTER XXIV

Orozco was dressed in torn sweater, patched trousers, and the cheapest kind of work shoes made from old tyres and canvas uppers. He faced Alvarez across the entrance hall of his house and waited with stolid patience.

'I thought I'd come and have a word with you,' said Alvarez.

Orozco continued to stare.

'Is there somewhere where we can sit?'

They went into the kitchen. There was a stone sink, fed by a single cold water tap, a bread oven fired by wood, a butane cooker, a wooden table, a cupboard, and two chairs. They sat, on opposite sides of the table.

'You fought in the war,' said Alvarez finally. 'You left the island an idealist and like all the other idealists you had your idealism shot away and by the time it was over you'd discovered only four things in life were really worthwhile: a hole to shelter in, water to drink, food to eat, and a friend for his friendship.'

'That's right,' said Orozco.

'A real man will always fight for what he knows to be essential. So you'd kill for possession of a hole, a filled water-bottle, a hunk of bread, or to protect a friend.'

'Maybe.'

'Who is your friend?'

Orozco shrugged his shoulders.

'He doesn't have to be someone who fought on the same side, does he? Just someone who fought, who felt death pass close by, who realized that the real cowards in any war are those who started it and keep it going with words. Luis fought for the other side. Maybe you even faced each other across no-man's-land and shot, hoping to kill. But that didn't make you enemies, that made you friends.'

Orozco stood up and walked over to the cupboard. He opened the right-hand door and reached inside to bring out a half-filled litre bottle, unlabelled. He put this down on the table. 'D'you want some?'

'I've drunk too much already this afternoon.'

'Only a ten-year-old who pisses his pants talks like that.'

'I'll never see forty again, so pour me one.'

Orozco went over to the sink and brought back two glasses. He dried them on a dirty cloth, pushed one glass and the bottle across the table. 'Pour your own.'

Alvarez half-filled his glass. 'The dog barked that first Thursday night. Barked and went on barking and howling. I reckoned it was kicking up a row because Señorita Cannon was creeping about the place, but she used to fuss it and feed it and if it had seen her it would maybe have barked a couple of times, but no more. So who was it barking at?'

Orozco poured himself out a drink.

'It was barking at Señor Freeman. He hated the dog and the dog hated him.'

They drank.

'Why didn't Matilde cook supper that night as it was a Thursday? Her day off was Monday. So why wasn't she there to cook the señor his esclatasangs after she'd checked them to make certain there wasn't a llargsomi among them?'

Orozco had already emptied his glass. He refilled it.

'Who knew she wasn't going to be there, so that a llargsomi could be put in among the esclatasangs and wouldn't be noticed since the Englishman would be doing his own cooking and he didn't know one from t'other? Señorita Cannon couldn't have known Matilde wasn't there and so she could never have believed she could poison the señor with a llargsomi.'

They were silent for a while. The room was beginning to darken so that Orozco's face, which was against the light, was no longer sharply featured.

'You had a row with the señor that Thursday. What was it about?'

'Seeds.'

'Don't be so bloody silly,' said Alvarez, as he gave himself a second drink. 'The Englishman had laid on a big seduction scene so that Señorita Cannon would walk in in the middle of it and be so shocked and disgusted that no one would be at all surprised when she committed suicide. It all worked out to begin with. Señorita Cannon was shocked and disgusted and did rush off in a hell of a state. But the other woman was also in a state and he hadn't reckoned on that. Veronica demanded to be taken back to her hotel, which left him very frustrated . . . I suppose he'd had his dirty eyes on Matilde for quite a time?'

Orozco muttered something.

'He was the kind of man who thought that just because he was rich and she was poor, she was fair game. So since Veronica had left him high and dry, he'd make do with her . . . She told you that afternoon that she'd had to fight him off, didn't she? And you promised her you'd deal with the trouble?'

'Luis had asked me to look after her,' said Orozco in a harsh voice.

'So how did you go about dealing with the situation?'

'I spoke to the señor in the garden. Understand this, I was polite, even though he had behaved like a dog which has scented a bitch. "Please," I said, "do not try to be friends with Matilde. She is married to Luis and is a good wife and it upsets her very much to be treated as a whore." He shouted and swore at me. Said it was no business of mine and to keep my dirty nose out of it if I wanted to keep my job.' He slammed his clenched fist down on the table. 'He spoke to me as if I were not fit to be spat on.'

'What happened next?'

'I saw Matilde and I told her I had spoken to the señor. I did not tell her how he had answered, but truly I thought he would now keep away from her because no man could act so shamefully as not to.' He slammed his fist down on the table again and the glasses rattled. 'I was here, eating, when Catalina from the store on the corner of the road came and said there was a telephone call for me from a woman who sounded very upset. I knew then what had happened. I ran to the shop and Matilde told me he had come again to the kitchen and had tried to kiss her and his hands began to tear at her dress. She cried to him to leave her alone and prayed to the Virgin Mary and when he became so busy pulling off her dress she escaped and ran up to her bedroom and locked herself in. I told her I would go to the house and take her to her cousin's. When I went with her to her cousin's, I told her it would never happen again.'

'Because you were going to kill him?'

'I did not tell her that,' he said simply.

'Why did you not just get in touch with Luis? Then he could have taken her away from the house and there would have been no need to kill.'

'Listen. Luis is much older than her and she is beautiful so always he keeps his eyes open in case a young man comes visiting. Hasn't it always been so with old husbands?

Suppose she had said, "The señor chased me twice and
the second time he tore off my dress before I could
escape"? Luis would have asked himself, why did the
Englishman chase her once? And why did he return a
second time even though she says she fought him off the
first time? Did she perhaps not fight hard enough? Has
she smiled at him because he is rich and young and her
blood is hot? Is the truth this, that they have spat on my
bed?'

'He wouldn't have begun to think like that if he really
loved her.'

Orozco spoke with angry sarcasm. 'So how big a fool
can a policeman be? Do you think an old husband with a
young and beautiful wife doesn't look at each young man
who comes near her and wonder? If Matilde had told
Luis everything, he would have listened and believed
today. But tomorrow there would have been a little worry
in his mind, and the next day that little worry would have
become a big one. And he would accuse her and she
would swear by the Holy Mother that she had never
smiled at the Englishman and he would believe her and
all would be all right. Until the next day when there
would be a little worry in his mind and as he stroked her
breasts he would wonder if the Englishman had stroked
them with warmer hands . . . Luis is my friend. I cannot
let him suffer this.'

'You seem so certain Luis would have been too jealous
to trust her. Why? Has he cause to be jealous, but doesn't
know it?'

Orozco pushed the bottle across. 'Drink.'

Alvarez refilled his glass.

'So?'

Alvarez looked at him and wanted to put his hands
around his shoulders and tell him that while there were
men who loved friendship and another's honour more

than life, the world could not be wholly rotten. 'Does Matilde know or does she only wonder?'

'Just wonders.'

'Then only you and I can be certain.' Alvarez drank. He put down his glass. 'The foreigners come here and they buy the houses so that peasants can no longer live in them and they waste the rich soil on flowers so that the peasants can no longer grow vegetables. With their money they distort all values until the young want everything and no longer know how lucky they are to have anything. But worst of all they bring corruption with them so that instead of honouring innocence and faithfulness they try to defile and debauch it . . . Let them wallow in their corruption.'

'What does that mean?'

'It means that the English señorita accidentally killed the señor, while he deliberately killed her. After all, what could be neater? Everything is taken care of.' He was silent for a while, then he said: 'Tell me, do you really believe that a younger wife who is not corrupted but is pure innocence will look at other men behind her husband's back?'

'Of course, if she is given the chance.'

'How can you be so cynically sure?'

'I was a young and handsome soldier. Once.'

Alvarez finished his drink. 'What a dirty, stinking world it sometimes is,' he muttered, with alcoholic despondency.

CHAPTER XXV

Ramón Mena was on the hard talking to one of his workmen when Alvarez came through the gateway of the boatyard. He greeted the other. 'Well, Enrique, what can I do for you? Sell you that twelve-million-peseta yacht you were so interested in?'

'Some other day. Right now I'd like a quick chat, if that's convenient?'

'Sure. Come along to the office so we can do our chatting over a drink.'

They walked into the main shed and passed between two boats, one of which was nearly completed. In his office, Mena pointed to the easy chair on the far side of the desk. 'Grab a seat while I find the bottle.' He looked in one cupboard, then turned to a second one. 'Lucia asked me only yesterday if I'd seen you recently and how were you? I said you were just as dissolute as ever.' He found the bottle he sought. 'Ever since my brother died, Enrique, Lucia has been thinking about another husband. Women love dissolute men because it gives them the chance to try to reform them, but she weeps too easily for you.' He filled two tumblers with brandy. 'Here you are – drink that up and tell me the news.' He sat down.

'First off, you tell me something. How's the Englishman getting on with you?'

'If I had a dozen like him, I'd have the best boatyard in Spain.'

'He's still working here?'

'Of course he is. Doing an ordinary bloke's job until he becomes a partner.'

'Oh!' Alvarez slowly shook his head in perplexity. He drank, then shook his head again.

Mena spoke with some asperity. 'Here, that's not fifty-peseta coñac, it's Carlos I, so why are you looking like that?'

'The cognac's velvet,' acknowledged Alvarez, yet if anything looking a shade more gloomily worried.

'Then what's eating you?'

'I'm worried about you.'

'Me? I'm fine except when someone sits opposite me drinking my best coñac and makes like it's homemade palo.'

'But how are we going to keep you out of trouble for breaking the labour acts? That's the problem.'

'Who's broken any labour acts?'

'The Englishman's a foreigner and he's working for you, yet he hasn't a work permit.'

Mena stared at Alvarez, disbelief slowly giving way to broad amusement. 'You old bastard!' he finally said. 'You really had me worried there, with your ugly old mug looking like the end of the world had happened five minutes ago.'

'But the work the Englishman is doing at the moment could as well be done by a Mallorquin, couldn't it?'

'Of course. D'you think I'm going to let him deal direct with the customers before he's a partner? I'm not that soft.'

'If a Mallorquin could do the work, then the Englishman wouldn't be granted a work permit.'

'Forget all this nonsense.'

Alvarez shook his head. 'You're breaking the law.'

'So? Am I going to be sent to jail for the rest of my life just because I employ one Englishman without a work permit? Who worries about such technicalities?'

'The law does.'

'Then you know what you can do with the law, don't you? Here, it's not like you to go on and on this way, moaning about something of no consequence.'

'Don't you understand? I'm worried for your sake. These days the government's making things really tough for someone who breaks the labour laws – because of all the unemployment. Call it a technicality if you like, Ramón, but I've seen real trouble come from no worse a breach of the law.'

'There are foreigners all over the island still being employed without work permits.'

'Because the law doesn't officially know about them.'

'And the law doesn't officially know about this one.'

'I know.'

Mena stared with sudden sharp enquiry at Alvarez.

Alvarez finished his drink. He wiped his mouth on the back of his hand. 'The big trouble comes afterwards. An employer commits a breach of the acts and gets fined a bit and he reckons that's an end to it. But it isn't, not by a long chalk. The inspectors start calling to make certain all the other million and one regulations are being observed and of course some of them aren't because who ever knows what they all are? Is there enough light and heat, are there proper safeguards, changing rooms, lavatories, showers . . . Your boatyard isn't all that up-to-date, is it? I'm worried that by the time the inspectors finish with it you'll have a bill for three or four million in improvements.'

Mena sat very upright and aggressively thrust his chin forward. 'What is this? A shake-down?'

'You surely know me better than that.'

'Then if it isn't, why go on and on telling me how disastrous things can get?'

'I'm trying to work out how best you can avoid them.'

'Tell me.'

'There could be a way, you know. Make Señor Anson a partner right off and then it's all over and done with. No one's going to get hot and bothered over what happened yesterday.'

'When he comes in this door with a million and a half, he's a partner.'

'Sure. Only he hasn't a million and a half and it looks like now he won't be able to get it.'

'He won't? Then he's unlucky.'

'Ramón, you know he's a first-class bloke and will bring a lot of new work to the yard. Why not give him the partnership now and let him pay you back over the years out of his income? With a proper rate of interest added, naturally.'

'Impossible! I must have the million and a half to expand and I must expand if I am to have a partner.'

'Yes, I can see that.' Alvarez sighed. 'Life is never as easy as it should be, is it?' Then he brightened. 'But here there is one way round the trouble.'

'Sure. He pays me the million and a half.'

'You say you need the money. But aren't you forgetting you already have it? Wasn't your wife left a finca? The one I've been told she's just sold to a German?'

'That's her money.'

'Understood. But surely she got more than she reckoned on because the German was a fool and didn't bargain? She'll have extra money that she won't have expected.'

'Who said she sold so well?'

'Is it a lie, then?'

Mena fiddled with his nose. 'There was, perhaps, a very little more than she originally thought she'd get.'

'Not the two million that people are saying you are boasting about?' Alvarez smiled companionably. 'Now what could be a better place to invest such extra money than in the future of your boatyard?'

'Listen, Enrique, I told Eduardo a million and a half and that's the price. I'd look soft if I climbed down now.'

'Generous, not soft. And who would hear about it if you didn't tell?'

'Why the hell should I do such a thing?'

'Because I reckon that at heart you like helping people. And also because you would be well advised to avoid the possibility of having to pay out three, could be as much as four, million on all those extra lights, heating, windows, lavatories . . .' Alvarez became silent.

Mena owed some of his success to the fact that he could make up his mind quickly. He made it up quickly now. He drained his glass, refilled it, then pushed the bottle across the desk. 'If I had to to do business with you, I'd sew up all my pockets first,' he said, a note of reluctant admiration in his voice. He studied Alvarez curiously. 'You must like Señor Anson a hell of a lot?'

'I hate his guts.'

'Why?'

'Because he's young.'

'Well, not even you can do anything about that. Here, fill your glass and drink up. Know something, Enrique? Face to face with you, I begin to feel quite virtuous.'

Alvarez filled his glass and drank.